Ripper's Ghost

By

Kennedy Welles

2014

Ripper's Ghost © 2014 Kennedy Welles
Triplicity Publishing, LLC

ISBN-13: 978-0990471691
ISBN-10: 0990471691

This is a work of fiction. Names, characters, places, and incidents are the product of the author's imagination and are used fictitiously. Any resemblance to actual persons, living or dead, business establishments, events of any kind, or locales is entirely coincidental. The portions of this work that are based on actual events are the author's interpretation of the events, and therefore fictitious.

Printed in the United States of America
First Edition – 2014
Cover Design: Triplicity Publishing, LLC
Interior Design: Triplicity Publishing, LLC
Editor: Morgan Woeste - Triplicity Publishing, LLC

Acknowledgements

I would like to thank Morgan, my editor, who worked diligently to correct my mundane mistakes.

Dedication

This book is dedicated to my grandmother, the person who showed me the joy of mysteries. Without her, I would not be reading books today, and I most definitely would not be writing them.

Nanna, here's one you can finally read!

25 FEBRUARY 2013

Cindy Smith hiked her short dress slightly higher, revealing more of her thigh as the gleam of headlights in the distance cast a glow on the darkened road ahead of her. She pushed her tiny breasts together and up towards the open collar of the tight dress. Then, she swung her long hair over her shoulder as she sashayed towards the curb, careful not to step in the pitted holes of the concrete with her high-heeled boots.

The dark car rolled to a stop. She checked for police in both directions and got in when she heard the lock click. She slid down into the bucket seat and closed the door. The lock clicked once again and the car sped away into the darkness. There were no interior lights in the car to illuminate the driver, but she proceeded anyway.

"What would you like me to do for you?" she said, reaching across the console towards his inner thigh.

The car rolled to a stop on a dark alley just off White's Row, a few blocks from the corner where she had been picked up.

"I want you to tell everyone I'm back," he said in a deep voice as he lurched across the console. Before she could react, he grabbed her frail body and twisted her to the side as he covered her face with a wet rag. He smiled as her small body went limp and slumped down against him.

He pushed her away and got out of the car. The moon was covered by thick, low-hanging clouds. It was barely two a.m. and the street was quiet, just the way he liked it. He opened the passenger door and pulled the woman's lethargic body from the car, laying her out flat on the sidewalk. Then hovered over her, drawing a pocket knife from the inside of his overcoat. He cursed the moon for shadowing itself tonight as he opened the blade and shoved it into the warm body below him. He punctured her lower abdomen and upper thighs with a handful of shallow wounds as if it were second nature. He took his time, placing them sporadically and watching the blood seep into her thin dress. Then, he wiped the blade on a clean area of her dress.

Satisfied, he stood up, folded the blade, and slipped it back inside his jacket pocket. He put the wet rag over her face once again when she began to stir and moan in pain.

Looking back at her body one last time, he grinned at the contrast of dark red blood pooling under her pale skin and soaking into the concrete.

28 MARCH 2013

Sheryl Smith was sitting in her brothel room near the Mile End Tube Station. She had just finished with her latest appointment and was in the process of redressing when she heard a soft knock at the door. Assuming he had left something in the room, she opened the door without looking through the peephole.

"I'm sorry, I don't think I have anymore appointments this evening," she said to the man standing in the doorway.

"This won't take long," he replied in a guttural voice as he moved inside the room, pushing the door closed with his foot. He grabbed her so quickly she was unable to scream.

He spun her around so that her back was against him. Holding her jaw closed tightly with hos hand and pinning her head against his shoulder, he reached into his pocket. He tried to look at the light gleaming from the edge of the blade, but once again he was in a sparsely light area, causing the blade to look dull and unfulfilling. He frowned.

She tried to move towards the bed to get a better look at him in the mirror over the dresser, but the man was solid and able to tighten his grip. She wished she could remember what he looked like when she opened the door. All she could think of was darkness, then pain, severe pain as her eyes closed.

He drove the knife into the side of her neck in one swift movement, then he pulled the blade away and shoved her to the floor as blood spurted from the wound . He watched her flopping on the floor while he wiped the blade clean on the wrinkled bedding. He smiled as he walked out of the room.

7 AUGUST 2013

Tracy Wright had just finished having a conversation with two friends. She had no more appointments for the night, so she decided to take a walk and get some air. Rounding the corner a block away from the brothel, she noticed a passing car slowing next to the curb. She often found men of high-class that paid well while walking the streets in the darkness. She wondered if it was the fear of being caught. Prostitution wasn't illegal but street soliciting was. Maybe that was why she did it, for the thrill.

Tracy walked over to the car and leaned down, expecting the window to open. Instead, she heard the distinct click of the door lock. Grabbing the handle, she swung the door open and slid inside. She could barely make out the features of the driver in the darkness as the car sped away.

He turned quickly down a side road and stopped.

Tracy smiled. "Good evening, fine sir. What is your pleasure tonight?" she said, reaching for his crotch in the darkness.

He snickered. "My pleasure is for you to die," he said in a low voice as he wrapped his arms around her, smothering her face with a wet rag. Her body relaxed against him and he pushed her towards the door, removing the rag from her face.

Checking the mirrors, he pulled back out on the main road and drove for a few miles before stopping in front of an abandoned building. He backed the car down the alley and parked next to an old side door that would have been used for discreet entrances and exits.

Tracy began to stir and he placed the rag over her face again. She calmed immediately. He walked around to the passenger side of the car and picked Tracy's limp body up, carrying her through the doorway into the darkened building and down a narrow corridor.

He turned through the doorway at the first door on the left and deposited her body onto the middle of the floor. The only furniture in the small room was a rickety antique steamer chest in the corner with a vintage oil lamp next to it. He removed his long black jacket and matching hat, placing them neatly near the doorway before walking over to the chest. He lit the lamp, casting a golden glow over the room. Glancing at the pale body in the center of the floor, he felt his blood rush to his gut. He took a few deep breaths to calm his excitement and opened the chest. An array of shiny razor sharp knives and daggers of all shapes and sizes were laying on satin cloth and strategically lined across the bottom of the shallow chest. He chose a penknife and a short dagger, looking at each one carefully in the light as the sharp edge gleamed. He smiled shyly as he moved each blade slowly over to see the shimmer on each side.

Satisfied with his choices, he hovered over Tracy's body and knelt down next to her. Taking the dagger in his hand, he made one swift move, shoving it through her

6

breast and into her heart. Warm red blood oozed from the wound. She jerked and flopped as he laid the dagger to the side and began stabbing from her throat to her groin with short strokes of the penknife. Blood began pooling on the floor around her. At the thirty-ninth thrust he stopped and wiped both knives clean on her clothes before standing up. He carefully put his knives away and closed the trunk. Tracy's body lay blood soaked and lifeless in the middle of the room as he stepped around her and walked down the hall.

He returned a few minutes later, picked the body up and carried her back outside, placing her inside the trunk of the dark car. The streets of London were deserted in the middle of the night, except for the stray prostitute here and there that defied the laws. He turned down Gunthorpe Street and came to a stop in front of Sunley House. Carefully, he removed the body from the trunk of his car and deposited it on the front steps. He got back into the car and smiled into the rearview mirror at the lifeless body as he disappeared into the night.

Chapter One

"Ms. Donovan, you have a package to sign for," Josie's bubbly voice echoed through the intercom.

Spencer Donovan looked around the walls of her office. Degrees and certifications covered one wall and bookcases and filing cabinets covered the others. She wondered who would have sent her a personal package. She was a District Attorney for the State of New York in the New York County District Office and a former Criminologist for the FBI.

Spencer never received personal mail at her office and wondered who was requesting her signature as she slipped her dark suit jacket on over the light colored blouse and walked out of her office. The young courier was standing by the reception desk shuffling back and forth on his feet obviously pressed for time and annoyed he had to wait so long for a signature.

"May I help you?" Spencer asked, walking up to him.

"I have a package for Spencer C. Donovan." he said to her.

"I'm Spencer Donovan," she replied.

"I need to see your I.D."

Spencer huffed, "What exactly am I signing for?"

"I can't give you any information until I see some identification. It's company policy for confidential deliveries."

Spencer tucked her chin length brown hair behind her ear in swift motion and waved for him to follow her down the hall. She wasn't about to waste her time walking all the way back to the reception desk again. As they entered her office, Spencer walked around her desk and opened the pocket on the side of her briefcase. She pulled her New York State Employee I.D. out, handing it to him. He checked the name and handed her a brown enveloped postmarked London, England. When the young man left, Spencer sat down in her leather chair, opening the envelope carefully.

Spencer Carlene Donovan of New York City, New York, born 1980

Ms. Donovan,

Your immediate presence is requested by Dr. Abner Montague PH.D at 27 White Church Lane, London E1 United Kingdom. This request is in regards to historical documentation relating to your biological family. This matter is of great importance and cannot be discussed over the telephone or Internet devices, which is why you are being summoned personally.

Sincerely,

A. Montague PH.D

Spencer stared at the letter, reading it once again before slipping it back into the envelope. There was no phone number on the letter and no return address on the envelope. She wondered if this was some kind of hoax. Most of everyone she knew was aware that she'd been adopted as a baby and her adopted parents died tragically close to ten years earlier. Her adopted parents didn't know anything about her birth mother or her biological family. She knew she had been adopted in Ireland and moved to America as a small child. She was unable to trace anything regarding her adoption or her family, so she finally gave up and moved on with her life after her parents passed away.

By the end of the day, Spencer was unable to concentrate on the pending cases on her desk and had read and reread the letter half a dozen times. Finally giving in, she booked a flight to London leaving the next morning.

Spencer pushed the intercom button and rolled her eyes when Josie bounced into her office with her bubbly personality in full swing.

"I will be out of the office for a few days. Please make the cancellations to my schedule beginning tomorrow."

"Yes, ma'am. Judge Perryman isn't going to be happy. You have a meeting with him tomorrow afternoon."

"I don't care about Judge Perryman. If he gives you any problems, tell him you know about his affair with that floozy he calls a secretary."

10

"Are you serious?" Josie stepped closer. She loved gossip and this was juicy information.

Spencer laughed. "No, Josie, you're so damn gullible. Just tell him a distant family member has passed away and I needed to go settle the trust."

"Does this have to do with that letter you got this morning?"

"Yes, I need to get going. I'll call you if my itinerary changes."

Josie nodded and walked out of the room. She was a good assistant, albeit a little airheaded. Her animated personality was somewhat uplifting, despite being annoying, and seemed to make the extremely dull days around the office tolerable. Spencer packed the letter and her laptop in her briefcase and walked out of the office.

Chapter Two

Spencer arrived in London after a seven hour non-stop flight and walked straight to the baggage claim area to wait for her small suitcase; while she waited she watched the evening news story on the nearby TV. When the reporter began talking about a murder, she stepped a little closer. Her criminology background with the bureau had led her to many crime scenes and homicide cases. A small part of her still missed the chill of a crime scene and the thrill of matching wits with a killer. The man on the TV was talking about an unidentified woman who had been stabbed multiple times and found dead a few weeks before in London's East End in the Whitechapel District.

The turn style squeaked as it began to move and luggage started trickling inside. Spencer tore her eyes from the new story in time to see her bag pass by. She grabbed it quickly and forgot all about the murdered woman as she stepped outside and hailed a cab. She gave the driver the address she had written down and leaned back in the seat.

"Are you going to the university, miss?" the driver asked.

"No," Spencer replied, staring through the window at the passing buildings.

"Are you here on holiday? The Whitechapel District and Ripper Tours usually attract a great number of tourists this time of year."

"Actually, I had no idea this was the same area. I'm going to meet someone about a family matter."

"It's not as troubled here as it once was, but there was a woman murdered nearby a few weeks ago. When news of the slaughtered woman spread, the tourism industry picked up in Whitechapel. Be careful walking around the district at night and I'd advise you to stay away from Hackney."

Spencer looked at the man in the mirror with a scruffy five o'clock shadow on his face and a worn pageboy hat on his head, and wondered if making this impromptu trip was going to be a huge waste of her time. Nodding at him, she turned her eyes back to the side window.

The car finally pulled alongside the curb and came to a stop next to a large brown building with multiple covered windows. Spencer paid the fare, tipping the man generously before getting out. She plucked the address out of her jacket pocket and looked for number twenty-seven. It was dark and the street lights barely illuminated the sidewalk in front of her. She quickly found the number she was looking for, stepped the couple of curbside stairs, and rang the bell.

After a minute or two she impatiently rang the bell again, wondering if maybe she should have sent a letter to the address informing this Abner Montague of her travel arrangements before actually traveling. Perhaps he was out for the evening.

"May I help you?" An older gentleman pulled the door open slightly. He was short in stature and slightly overweight in the middle, but not enough to be labeled as round. He had a thin grey ambassador style handlebar mustache that matched his hair. He was dressed in a dark blue suit with matching waist coat, trousers, and vest, complimented by a white shirt with a red and blue paisley tie. The air around him smelled of cherry tobacco.

Spencer blinked her eyes clearing her throat. She felt as if she just saw the door to the nineteenth century open right in front of her. "I'm looking for Dr. Abner Montague," she said.

"And you are?"

"Oh, I'm sorry. My name is Spencer Donovan."

The man took a step back and eyed the woman at the door. She was dressed in a dark ladies pantsuit with a light colored blouse. She was his height, maybe a little taller with the heels on her shoes. Her eyes were as green as an Irish meadow. Her brown hair barely touched the collar of her jacket and was neatly tucked behind her ear on one side more than likely her more favorable side. The woman standing in front of him was unmistakably American.

"Do I have the correct address?" Spencer asked, taking a step back to check the building number and reread the address on the paper in her hand. "Is this twenty-seven White Church Lane?"

"Indeed it is," he said opening the door widely. "I am Abner Montague. Please come inside Ms. Donovan."

Spencer hesitated before walking inside. The small room was cluttered with bookcases that wrapped almost completely around the entire room, blocking the windows. A large dark colored desk was covered in papers on one side of the room with two small antique leather chairs in front of it. A stack of locking filing cabinets lined the wall adjacent to the desk. There was another smaller desk on the other side of the room, sitting in front of one of the bookcases and covered with boxes.

"Welcome to my office," he said, holding his hand out to one of the seats in front of the desk. Spencer heard the lock click as he shut the door behind her. "I wasn't expecting you to arrive in such a timely manner," he said, sitting in the old wingback chair across from her.

"Forgive me for being blunt, but how is it that you seem to know about my biological family Dr. Montague?"

He grinned. "Americans, you're always straight to the point," he replied opening the top drawer of his desk. He pulled a piece of paper and a pen out, laying them in front of him.

"Do you mind if I see your identification? This is matter of great historical importance and I'd hate for this information to get into the wrong hands," he said.

Spencer shook her head, wanting to laugh at all of the secrecy as she flashed her U.S. Government I.D.

"Thank you, Ms. Donovan. What do you know about your biological family?"

"Nothing. That's why I'm curious to know how you even know who I am."

He slid the paper across the desk to her. "This is a confidentiality clause. I need you to sign this."

Spencer glared at the man. She didn't like the Agent 007 act he was putting on. "I sincerely hope you're not wasting my time."

"Ms. Donovan, the information that I am about to share with you could put you and I both in extreme danger and I need to know you will keep this information to yourself in strict confidentiality. I'm an honest and trustworthy man. My family has kept this information secret for one-hundred and twenty-five years and I plan to continue its secrecy."

Spencer raised an eyebrow. She had a feeling she was about to go on a wild goose chase at the expense of some crazy British kook. She scratched her signature across the line at the bottom and handed the form back to him.

"Splendid," he said, rising from his seat. "Please follow me and watch your step."

Spencer watched him go through a small brown door the opened to a single narrow staircase. "Where are we going?"

"Up to my flat."

"What the hell for?" Spencer asked nervously. As a criminologist she'd learned the ins and outs of the minds of crazy people and killers and as a prosecutor she'd dealt with them on a daily basis. This Abner Montague was definitely starting to ping her radar screen.

"The information I am going to share with you is kept in a fireproof safe in my flat. It has been passed down from generation to generation in my family and is of great value."

Spencer shook her head and followed him up without saying anything. The room at the top of the stairs opened up into a large studio room with various shades of brown furniture all over. She came to the conclusion that brown was the man's favorite color, either that or he was colorblind. Classical music was playing softly on the antique record player in the corner. She recognized it as a Mozart Piano Concerto.

"Please have a seat. I'll return in just a moment," he said, disappearing behind a room divider that obviously hid his bed and dressing area.

Spencer sat nervously in a plain brown chair and glanced around at the old pictures on the wall that seemed to take her on a historical tour of London for at least a hundred years. She wondered how old the man really was.

He returned quickly with a thick file folder and turned the record player off. Sitting down across from her, he laid the folder on the table.

"Would you care for some tea?" he asked, turning towards the tea cart next to the chair he was sitting in. He poured himself a cup, dropping one sugar cube and a splash of milk into the brown liquid.

"No, thank you," she answered without looking up. Her eyes were drawn to the curiosity of the folder laying in front of her.

"Ms. Donovan, you may not believe what I am about to tell you, and honestly I wouldn't believe it either if I hadn't done some of the research myself. I am a historian and a true crime novelist. I am also a history professor at the nearby London University. Hence all of the books down in my office. I often have students come by and that is what I keep this information locked away. "My great-great-grandfather, Allaster Montague, was a lawyer in the Whitechapel District, actually not too far from where we are right now. Of course, his office building is long gone today.

"In late 1888, I believe sometime in the month of December, a man came in wanting him to hold a sealed document for a family member. Allaster was used to keeping last will and testaments, land deeds, and other important documents so he agreed. The man had very specific instructions. The letter was to be given to the heir of Abigail Franklin in the year two-thousand and thirteen. My great-grandfather thought the man had possibly escaped the mental asylum, but nevertheless, he kept the wax-sealed envelope. He described the man as being slightly taller than average with thick dark hair, dark eyes, and pale skin. He wore a black bowler hat and matching cloak over an informal black suit.

"My great-great-grandfather passed the information about this letter down to my great-grandfather Abbott Montague when he was close to the end of his years. Abbott had worked with his father for a number of years as a lawyer in the family business, never knowing of the secret letter until much later. Not long after Allaster Montague passed away, my great-grandfather was visited by a man in his later years that was seemingly checking in on the letter. He never gave his name and only told Abbott the person receiving the letter would also be an heir to Mildred Franklin. My great-grandfather described him as being a well-fit older gentleman with a little bit of grey in his hair and tall with dark features. He wore a black boiler hat and dark frock coat with a black knotted tie. He left quickly and never returned. That was the year 1912.

"My grandfather Adolph Montague came to know of the letter a few years after the birth of my father, Alfred Montague. My great-grandfather Abbott passed away weeks after revealing the information to my grandfather which happened to be a year before I was born. My grandfather was also a lawyer following in the family business. When I was a small child he told me the stories his father told him about the mysterious man and his letter. He believes he met the man once in 1914 when he came one last time to check on the letter. My grandfather was in the office visiting his father when an older gentlemen in a dark suit and hat came in. He was using a walking cane. When he saw that my grandfather had someone in his office, he excused himself before my grandfather ever saw him and never returned.

"When my father grew into a man and went to university, my grandfather told him of the secret letter and it's past, he remembered meeting the man and was intrigued, so my father changed his studies to become a historian. Later in his years, he became a history professor. It took my father many years to locate any information about Mildred Franklin or Abigail Franklin. He nearly made it his life's work.

"Twenty-five years ago my father and I began piecing together the descendants of these women and followed the lineage from the birth of Abigail Franklin in late 1888. That bloodline was traced all the way to America in the year 1988. " He paused to sip his tea.

"I'm still not sure how all of this pertains to me. Are you and I related, Dr. Montague?"

Abner smiled. "No, Ms. Donovan, you and I are not related. I'm afraid your distant relatives are much more intriguing than mine."

"So you're saying I'm related to Abigail Franklin, then."

"Yes."

"Who is Mildred Franklin?" she asked.

Abner pulled a paper chart from the file and unfolded it on the table in front of them. "Abigail had a daughter named Mildred Franklin in London in 1910. It is believed that the man that brought the letter to my great-great grandfather was Abigail's father and Mildred's grandfather."

"I'm still not sure how all of this adds up to me. I was born in Ireland, Mr. Montague."

Abner raised a hand to pause her. "Mildred had a daughter named Evelyn Porter in London in 1941. Mildred was very low class and endured a life of poverty as a lady of the night, just as her mother had. Evelyn too became a lady of the night and in her later years gave birth in London in 1980. That child whom she named Carlene was taken away to Ireland and adopted to an Irish couple that later moved to the United States." Abner watched the color change on Spencer's face.

"Are you saying I'm that child?" she whispered.

"It is without a doubt true. Your parent's kept Carlene, your birth name, as your middle name."

"How were you able to trace all of this?" she asked.

"Historical lineage and genealogy go hand in hand. This mystery has been in family as I said for 125 years."

"All of this for a letter? I don't understand it." Spencer studied the chart.

"It's not just any letter, Ms. Donovan. My family has believed all along that it's a letter from *him.*"

"Him? Him who?" She rubbed her temples where her head ached. She was still trying to grasp the fact that this man knew her family tree and her mother, grandmother, and great-grandmother were apparently all whores.

"It's late, maybe we should continue this in the morning, Ms. Donovan," Abner said.

"You're probably right. I need some time to digest all of this information." Spencer stood up. "Is there a hotel nearby? I left in such a haste I forgot to book a room."

Abner shook his head. "You definitely do not want to stay in this area or go out looking for a room this time of night. You may sleep here on my sofa. I'll take you into the city in the morning where you can book a proper room."

"I heard on the evenings news that a woman was murdered recently. My cab driver said it was close by."

"Yes. Yes, it was. Just past the university. The police haven't been specific to the exact location, but I know where it was. There is much more information I need to share with you in the morning." He handed her blankets and a pillow.

"The washroom is next to the kitchenette. Please let me know if you need anything. I'm a light sleeper."

"Thank you," she said, taking the offering and sitting down on the couch.

In the last twenty-four hours, Spencer's life had turned upside down. She wasn't sure if there was any truth to what the Victorian Era looking professor had said to her, but it seemed to make sense nonetheless. She was too tired from the long flight and jet lag to think much more about it. If the old man's story didn't pan out in the morning, she'd simply hop back on a plane and go home, wasting two and a half of her vacation days.

31 AUGUST 2013

Delilah Anderson was in her mid-forties, but appeared at least ten years younger. Due to her lack of rent money for the week she was eager to get the night started and had no qualms about who she picked up for the evening. As she turned the corner of her walking path she was snatched back into the darkness by strong arms. Her face was covered by a wet rag, before she could scream everything went dark.

When she woke up again she was lying on the floor in a dark room. She turned her head towards the flickers of light coming from a lamp in the corner and could barely make out the shadow of a man as he walked towards her.

"What are you going to do to me?" she whispered.

He smiled. "You have the privilege of being my Mary Nichols," he said. Kneeling over her, he placed the wet rag on her face once more.

He went back to the chest in the corner. Looking at each glistening piece of metal, he chose a knife making sure it gleamed brightly in the light. Then, he smiled at the image of himself in the mirrored blade, and knelt over her again. Holding her head still with his hand over her face, he sliced the knife deeply across her neck severing the arteries and tissue down to the vertebrae. Blood sprayed to each side and poured from the corners of the wound. He wiped the knife across her chest to clean the blade as moved down her body and slid her dress up.

He stuck the knife in her once again making several jagged slices across her lower abdomen and few deep gashes downward on her lower right side. He wiped the knife and made one last slice completely across her abdomen disemboweling her.

He packed his knife away in the chest, wiped the sweat from his brow, and watched the blood ooze from her wounds until it was barely a trickle. He delicately placed her body into the trunk of the dark car parked outside and drove towards Durward Street.

The car came to a stop just outside of Kempton Court and slightly passed the school. He pulled the body from the trunk and placed her on the sidewalk with her legs stretched out and her dress pulled slightly up. He reached down and pushed her eyelids open widely. He grinned proudly and checked the street for signs of movement before getting back into his car.

Chapter Three

Spencer awoke in a strange place, nearly forgetting where she was at first. The smell of cherry tobacco permeated the air. She sat up, pushing the blanket to the end of sofa as she swung her feet to the floor.

"Dr. Montague?" she called out.

"Down here, Ms. Donovan," Abner said.

Spencer took her small travel bag into the bathroom, changed her clothes, washed her face, and brushed her teeth. She ran the hairbrush through her hair and tucked it neatly behind her ear on the left side.

"Ah, there you are," Abner said when she emerged from the washroom. "Would you care for some tea and biscuits?"

"If that is the equivalent to coffee and a bagel, I'm in," she said, setting her bag down next to the sofa. She noticed he had already removed the blanket and pillow that she'd slept on.

Abner grinned and chewed the corner of his handlebar mustache. He looked a decade younger in the daylight. He was dressed in another tailored pantsuit, dark grey this time with a black tie and white shirt. He walked over the kitchenette and returned with a tray of something that resembled bagels. He set the tray next to the tea cart and once again sat down in the chair that he'd occupied the night before, with the folder in his hand.

Spencer spread some sort of jelly substance on a biscuit and added an extra lump of sugar to her tea. She'd gladly murder someone for a cup of Starbuck's coffee with a double shot at the moment, but this would have to do.

"Last evening, I left off at the point of the letter." He drew a clear plastic sheath from the back of the file folder. A thin envelope with a red wax seal was in the middle. The paper looked like antique parchment.

Abner handed Spencer a pair of white silk gloves and he also put on a pair of the same gloves.

"This letter hasn't been touched since 1888. When the man returned to check on it in 1912 it was already placed in this protective cover."

"Why is this letter so significant?" Spencer asked.

"What do you know of London's history? Especially around the year 1888?"

Spencer thought for a minute then looked up at Abner's beady brown eyes. She looked down at the letter and back at his eyes. "You're not saying...that's not...I don't believe you."

"Ms. Donovan, a man fitting the vague description of the person that placed this letter into my great-great grandfather's hands was a horrid serial killer that terrorized London during the fall of 1888. My family has always believed this letter to be the work of his hand."

"So let me get this straight. You think my great-great grandfather was Jack the Ripper?" she laughed.

"Yes, indeed I do. I believe very much that this letter was written by him."

"I guess we should read it then," Spencer went to open the cover, but Abner stopped her. "I do believe it is addressed to me. Is it not?" she said.

"I'm sorry, Ms. Donovan. It's just that this letter has been in my family's possession for so long, I feel responsible for its safety."

"Fine, you open it," she huffed.

Abner slowly peeled the cover back and slid the envelope out into his hand. He used a thin metal letter opener to lift the wax seal and push the top fold of the envelope back. He reached inside with a pair of tweezers and pulled the letter out. Only touching the corners, he unfolded it, laying it out flat on the table. The parchment was flaky and the red ink was faded but still legible.

Dear Child,

If my instructions were carried out, you are viewing this letter some 125 years after I scribed it. I do not know you, although you shall know me through your history books. I wish to tell you my story, for you see, it was the thought of you that put my hands to rest. I am the man they seek in the year 1888. They will never catch me, I am too clever for them. It's become a jolly good laugh watching the hounds of Scotland Yard chase their wagging tails while I cover the streets of Whitechapel in red. Maybe they will soon understand whores have no place in this world with their filthy lying souls murdering innocence and spreading disease. I am no butcher nor doctor, simply a man scorned of hatred.

Forgive me, Child, for I have gone off topic. I have penned this letter to you, whomever you are, to finally put the legend to rest. A woman by the name of Abigail Bigsby, she once was a striking woman with a beautiful soul, until the day she informed me that she aborted my child to continue her role as a lady of the night. It is the hatred of that woman and her neediness to kill that sent me into the streets of London's East End. I was never able to find Abigail again and took my anger and frustration out on the women I encountered in the streets. These women paid over and over for what Abigail did to me.

A woman, high up in years, made her presence at my pub table just this day, to inform me that Abigail had given birth to my child a few weeks past, a baby girl she named Abigail Franklin. She had left Little Abby in the woman's care before returning to raise the child on her own. The woman notified me of her last known address.

On this evening, I saw my child for the first time and in that child's eyes, I saw a new legacy. Therefore, I have rested my hands knowing that one day whomever you are, you will know the legend of me and now understand the legacy I created for you.

Jack the Ripper

Spencer backed away from the table, staring at the faded red ink on the paper in front of her. She drew in a deep breath and cleared her throat.

"I think it's a hoax," she said.

"It's certainly not what I expected, but a hoax I think not." He removed his glasses and cleaned the lenses before placing them back on his face. He read the letter once again.

"Why would Jack the Ripper write a letter to his descendent 125 years later? None of that makes any sense. In fact, none of what you are telling me makes any sense." Spencer got up and walked over to the window.

"JTR did many things for reasons unknown. For instance, there were multiple murders in Whitechapel between 1888 and 1891. There are only five that are said to be his work. This letter has actually answered many questions that have arose over the decades. Why did he start? Why only five? Why were his murders so vicious? Why did he progress? How could someone in the year 1888 know all of this information if it wasn't himself penning this letter?"

"It still doesn't mean he is related to me if this is even written by him."

"There's more," Abner replied.

"What do you mean there's more?" Spencer turned from the window to face him.

"Do you believe in ghosts?" he asked.

"Ghosts? No," she sighed in frustration.

"Come with me," he said, walking down the stairs.

Spencer followed.

Abner checked the lock on his office door before sitting behind his desk. He opened a file laying on the desk and turned on his laptop. As it booted up, he packed a wad of tobacco into an old English smoking pipe and lit it. Cherry flavored tobacco smoke permeated the air, reminding Spencer of her grandfather in Ireland.

"I mentioned other murders during the same time period that supposedly weren't Jack the Ripper's hand. Those same murders have been repeating themselves this year."

"What do you mean repeating themselves? You mean a copycat?"

"No, I mean the killer has returned 125 years later. The killings are almost too precise too be done by any other hand than the original. I'm afraid we will soon know for sure," he said, puffing on pipe.

"Why? What's happening?"

"Last night marked the 125th anniversary of Jack the Ripper's first murder, a woman named Mary Nichols. Although, some historians do believe he started with a woman named Martha Tabram and if that's the case he has returned. The woman's body that was found a few weeks ago matches the same description of Martha Tabram's murder and the body was found in the same place exactly 125 years to the day. It's no coincidence, Ms. Donovan."

"Are you saying a ghost is now killing people?" She massaged her temples and couldn't remember the last time she had a headache this bad. This man was literally driving her mad.

"No, I don't believe in ghosts either. But, someone is out there posing as a ghost and I believe you are the only one that can stop him."

"Me? What makes you think I can stop some crazy killer?"

"I've read your cases. I know your work as a criminologist. I've been following you for a few years. I had to know for sure you were the person I was to seek out."

"Great, you've been stalking me."

"Not stalking, only following your career."

"This has been fun and all, but I really need to get going. I have real killers to put behind bars and although your theories sound interesting, that's just it, they are theories. I'm seeking the truth and you fooled me, Dr. Montague. You, sir, are no Sherlock Holmes and I am not your Watson. Now, if you will kindly call me a cab, I will be waiting out front." Spencer went upstairs, grabbed her bag, and walked back down to the front door.

"I do wish you would reconsider, Ms. Donovan. I have not lied to you. Everything I have shared with you is the truth based on my family's honor. My family would not have gone to the trouble of preserving that letter for all of these decades and tracing the path of the intended reader for the same amount of time. I'm sorry you feel as if I have wasted your time."

"Goodbye, Dr. Montague," Spencer said when she saw the taxi coming up the street.

Chapter Four

Spencer paid for a sandwich and a cup of coffee and found a seat near the gate her plane was taking off from. She had a three hour wait before her scheduled departure and her mind kept returning to the letter and mysterious murder from a few weeks earlier. She didn't believe any of Abner Montague's story. How could she? The more she thought about it, the more some of it made sense, but the facts were still very vague. She lived her life based on facts, not assumptions.

"Oh my word. Not again," An older woman sitting a few seats down was holding her chest as she watched the news on the big screen TV.

Spencer looked up at the TV, nearly spilling the cup of hot coffee she was holding when the words: *Another Whitechapel Murder, Jack the Ripper's Ghost has Returned* scrolled across the bottom of the screen. She grabbed her belongings and moved closer to the TV.

"Another body has appeared in London's Whitechapel District. This one on the 125th Anniversary of Mary Nichols murder at the hands of Jack the Ripper.

There are no details yet on the exact location the body was found or weapon used," said the reporter.

"Do you believe in ghosts?" the woman sitting close by said to Spencer.

"No," Spencer stood and grabbed her bag, thankful she decided not to check it this time.

She tossed her sandwich in the trash and sipped her coffee as she walked towards the airport exit, grabbing the first cab she saw waiting in line. She gave him Abner's address and quickly called the airline to cancel her flight as the car drove through the city.

"Are you sure you want to go into Whitechapel, miss? There have been two women murdered, one as recently as last evening."

"Yes, I am aware. It's fine." She smiled at him in the mirror.

~

Abner pulled the door open before Spencer could ring the bell. He'd anticipated her return. Whether she believed his story or not, her intriguing mind would bring her back. He nodded and removed the pipe from his mouth when she entered his office.

"I've been expecting you," he said.

"What made you think I would return?"

"You're curious, Ms. Donovan. You solve mysteries and this is the biggest mystery of your life, literally. I knew you would return. When I saw the news break the story on the poor murdered woman's body found last evening, I knew your return would be sooner than later. I made a kettle of fresh tea. Would you care for a cup?"

"No, I had coffee in the airport."

"Dreadful stuff," Abner said, visibly shaking his head as he poured himself another cup of tea. "Where shall we start?" he asked when he sat behind his desk.

"What do you know about these Whitechapel murders? I would like to go through everything and build a profile of who Jack the Ripper was and maybe we can use it to catch this ghost person before he kills anymore women." Spencer grabbed a pen and a notepad from her bag.

Abner pulled a group of files from the cabinet and set them on the desk in front of her. "This is everything pertaining to the murders that supposedly weren't Jack the Ripper and I also have multiple files on the murders he supposedly committed. Every woman that was attacked was a prostitute. They were all around forty years old, give or take a few except the last one, Mary Kelly. She was much younger, only twenty-five."

Spencer took her note pad and began making a timeline of the murders as Abner introduced her to every victim.

"If this person is truly copying these murders, then he attacked at least two people before killing the first girl. Now, he's killed his second. In that case, we really aren't looking at Jack the Ripper we are looking at all of the Whitechapel murders combined."

"Yes, that is true. Many people even back then believe that JTR was responsible for more than just the canonical five victims. Evidence wasn't collected and treated in the same manner that it is today and in 1888 they didn't have DNA or fingerprinting. Just about every investigation was solved by word of mouth or witnesses on the streets. These murders all happened to be unseen and unheard."

"Why aren't the police here putting out more information to warn people, especially women, to get off the streets at night?"

"Just like in 1888, they don't want the city in a uproar."

"That's just ludicrous. So they just let him go on killing people until they figure out who he is? If America worked that way we'd be up to our ears in dead bodies."

Abner shrugged. "That's the English way, so it seems."

"Do you know anything about these recent murders? Were they prostitutes?" She began making columns on her notepad.

"I'm not sure. The only thing they are saying in the news is two women have been found murdered. They aren't giving exact location details either. Although, I suspect they are being dumped at the ripper sites and are more than likely ladies of the night," Abner said.

"If the timeline is correct, we have a week before he strikes again. I need to read these files so I can get up to speed. I wasn't much of a Ripper fan so I chose other killers to study while I was at college."

"That makes sense. I'm sure you didn't think you would find out one day you were related to him."

"We don't know that for sure. In fact, all of that information sounds too fixed to be true in my opinion."

"You're surely entitled to your opinion, although facts speak for themselves. You can go upstairs and use my flat if you like or we can clear off that desk over there and you can work down here with me."

"Thank you, I'll use the desk."

"Can I ask you why you want to do this?" Abner handed her the files.

"You were right, Dr. Montague. If you truly know my background, then you know I am intrigued by mysteries that are nearly unsolvable. I need you to do something for me. You're a historian and know all about genealogy, correct?"

"Yes, that is correct."

"I need you to dig up everything you can on every member of that so-called family tree you have of me. Research everything about every person starting with Evelyn Porter. If you and I know this information, someone else may know too. I seriously doubt Jack the Ripper was my great-great grandfather, but if this new killer knows this story too and is somehow related to me, I'd feel awful if I didn't use my skills and knowledge to stop him."

"That is very possible," he said, clicking on the notes he had saved on his laptop.

Spencer went to work clearing the desk. She quickly set up her laptop and made a spreadsheet as she flipped open the first file. Her adrenaline flowed as she made notes on everyone's date of death, causes of death, and body location. She loved the rush and excitement she got from working a case and had missed it since leaving the FBI.

~

Hours later, Spencer had a small timeline built with details of each murder. She also had side notations of differences and similarities.

"The first women were attacked but not killed. One was stabbed in the torso and legs, and the other was stabbed in the throat," Spencer said.

"That is correct. Annie Millwood and Ada Wilson survived their attacks."

"The third woman, Emma Smith, was supposedly attacked by a gang or at least that's what she told the hospital when she was being tended to. She can be crossed off the list."

"It's rumored she was lying because she was a prostitute," Abner said.

"I disagree with that. I'm going to put her aside for now. I think Annie Millwood and Ada Wilson were trial runs. Maybe he wasn't sure what would work and was testing out the waters."

"Good call," Abner agreed. "It's always been my theory he progressed on his own and wasn't a doctor like everyone said he was. According to that letter, if it's true, he wasn't a doctor anyway. What do you think of the others?" he asked, relighting his pipe.

"Why was Mary Kelly chosen? I hate to jump right to the last victim, but this murder is very significant. You're right she was definitely much younger than the others. She was also killed inside her room and completely mutilated." She circled Mary's name on her notepad and smiled when she glanced over at him. Abner looked like Professor Plum, puffing his pipe in the study.

"Why do you think he treated her differently? All of the others were sliced up and dumped in the dirty streets."

"I think he knew she was the last one. She was his masterpiece. That's why he took hours with her and left her where he killed her. It was like artwork to him," she said, moving back to her computer screen.

"Ms. Donovan, would you like to break for dinner? We can order in if you'd like," Abner said.

"Please call me Spencer and yes, food would be wonderful. I'm starving, but I want to get this timeline completed. I pretty much eat anything, so whatever you chose is fine with me." Spencer went back to the file lying next to her laptop.

Chapter Five

Spencer spent another restless night on Abner Montague's couch. She needed to really think about getting a hotel room if she planned to stay in London. She wasn't sure how much longer she could sleep on his lumpy couch. She was beginning to think three nights was well past her limit and definitely overstaying her welcome.

"I was able to find a coffee house for you," Abner said, walking into the flat. "I also got some fresh biscuits."

"You're a lifesaver, Abner," Spencer exclaimed, reaching for the cup of coffee. It wasn't the best tasting brew, nevertheless, she drank it with a smile.

"What's the plan for today?" Abner questioned as he walked across the flat to store the bedding from the couch.

"I was thinking of taking one of those Ripper Tours. I also need to pick up a local map."

"Those tours are awful. Most of the sites have been rebuilt with other buildings, so nothing generally looks the same. I will take you around to the sites myself if you'd like and there is a map in my desk drawer you can have."

"Wonderful. When can we get started?" Spencer asked.

"After tea and biscuits," Abner said, sitting across from her with his cup of tea.

"Of course," she replied sarcastically. "Where exactly is that map? If you don't mind, I'd like to pick up where I left off last night."

"You American's are always so impatient," Abner huffed, shaking his head as he stood up and walked towards the staircase.

"Well, we only have a handful of days before this killer strikes again and I'd like to get a step ahead of him. You can go back to your precious tea in a minute."

Abner unfolded a large map across the top of his desk and took out a red pen.

"Here are the canonical five sites of Jack's murders," he said, making five small red circles in various areas of the map. "You'll have to look up the exact location of the others in the files I gave you. "

"Perfect. Thank you, Abner," she replied sincerely.

He went back upstairs and she began thumbing through her notes. She searched the top drawer of his desk for another pen color and began circling the other victim's locations with a blue pen. She was surprised to see the resemblance of a triangle. She'd read somewhere in the files that there was indeed a triangle and based on the theory she was working on, JTR definitely worked in the area he more than likely lived in.

When Abner appeared in the doorway, Spencer looked up from the map.

"I have a few ideas I want to run by you. I agree that Jack didn't know the victims. I think they were all random, maybe just in the right place at the right time. Each kill was obviously more detailed than the prior, probably because he was getting more comfortable, which is why Annie Chapman's intestines were thrown over her shoulder and her entire womb was missing from the body."

"There was never a trace of the missing body parts. Why do you think he took them? What's the justification?"

Spencer sighed. "I hate to keep going back to that damn letter in your safe. I only wish I hadn't read it beforehand. Still, if you remember back, the author of the letter states that his anger and rage were fueled by the supposed abortion of his child. It could be that the lower abdomen stabbings with the other victims and the removal of this victim's womb could indicate the letter to be somewhat truthful. He's obviously vindictive to that area of the body purposefully," she finished.

"That is a very strong possibility," Abner agreed, looking at multi-colored circles on his map.

"The night he killed the two women in late September is a fluke of nature. He has just sliced Elizabeth Stride's throat when something happened, forcing him to stop. She was murdered outside of a club-house, correct?"

"Yes. It was actually a print house that let the International Working Men's Education Society use a portion of their building for club meetings and entertainment. Stride's body was found by the gate in the courtyard at the side of the building. It was an area not often used by club members as it was usually locked and most people came and went from the front door. What are your thoughts on that night?" Abner asked.

"It was noisy, easy for him to kill her, but there were people around, at least twenty to thirty that evening, and someone must have come close to the area causing him to flee without carrying out his plans."

"In the inquest file you will see a deposition from a man named Diemshutz. Did you read it?"

"Yes, I did. He was the one with pony. He arrived at one a.m. and discovered the body. Just before that, around a quarter to one, a man and woman were seen together in the same area. It's possible that was JTR and Stride. If so, he had just enough time to subdue her before the man arrived with his pony. This is more than likely what caused Jack to leave in haste without finishing. This probably perturbed him in such a manner causing him to go in search of another victim. This idea would coincide with the Saucy Jack postcard which has handwriting very similar to the Dear Boss letter."

"I agree. We will come back to that. Why Mitre Square? It was outside of Whitechapel and away from his so-called killing zone."

"Easy," Spencer said, pointing to the map. "If someone was in the area when he killed Stride then there was the possibility she would be discovered. He had to go away from the area. In fact, he had to go away from the Metro Police. He walked for about ten minutes and ended up in Mitre Square. It's possible Catherine Eddowes was already there walking the street and became an easy target."

"According to testimony in Eddowes inquest, Edward Watkin walked the beat through Mitre Square at one-thirty a.m. and saw nothing, but on his pass of the same area at one-forty-four he discovered Eddowes body. Her intestines were around her shoulders and next to her left arm and her face had multiple cuts on her eyelids, her cheeks, and part of her nose was cut off. Her abdomen was cut in such a manner as to lay her open. Multiple organs were cut or punctured and the left kidney was completely removed. What are your thoughts here?" Abner said.

Spencer went to the desk she was using and returned with her notes. "I think the facial destruction is because he possibly thought he was seen with his last victim and there was an obvious account of a man and a woman being seen and then the obvious manner in which he left so rapidly. Maybe he cut her nose off because she was in the city and considered higher classed. I don't know," she shrugged.

"I do believe had some kind of medical knowledge to be able to pull off what he did to her out in the open in a very short amount of time. We're talking about fifteen minutes, most doctors couldn't remove someone's kidney in fifteen minutes plus do everything else he did. Do I think he was doctor? No. He could have studied medicine and maybe even worked as a coroner at one time. He gained his medical knowledge on his own and more than likely not through a university."

Abner nodded. "Interesting. There have been a number of people over the years that have said he could have been a medical assistant or coroner of some sort. Many believe he wasn't a doctor. If you go by that dreaded letter once again, he says he was not a doctor and if I recall he found it comical that the police would think so."

"Yes, we do keep coming back to that damn letter don't we?" Spencer agreed.

"Why do you think he took the kidney?" Abner asked.

Spencer shrugged. "For the life of me I cannot come up with a plausible explanation for that. It doesn't fit any scenario I have worked in my head. I have the same result for the message found on Goulston Street near the torn piece of bloody apron. If you match that to the From Hell letter you will note the misspellings and improper grammar thusly written by a poor, uneducated person. One could conclude these are written by the same hand, yet the Dear Boss letter and our letter are very similar and legibly written using proper spelling and grammar seemingly that of an educated man. The only conclusion is that this is all the handwriting of Jack the Ripper. He is highly educated and a bit of a jokester if you will. Writing different messages in different ways is his idea of throwing off the police that are already miles and possibly years away from catching him to begin with."

Abner lit his cherry tobacco pipe and sat down behind his desk. "Now, that is a theory I've never heard of. It is definitely possible, yes. But, then why the kidney?"

"Maybe to add to his little ploy with the police," she said.

"You're obviously a very educated woman, Spencer. I do believe you may be on the right track with your profile and investigation. If only you were part of Scotland Yard a hundred and twenty-five years ago." He smiled and puffed on his pipe.

"Well, if I couldn't catch him, maybe I can use him to catch his ghost," she replied.

Chapter Six

Spencer was sitting at the desk, working on her profile of Jack the Ripper and his victims while listening to the rain pound the windows, when Abner burst through the door from the street soaking wet.

"I was wondering where you were. You look like a drowned rat," she said. "I've been working on Mary Kelly's case and I wanted to run some theories by you."

"That can wait," he said, shaking the rain off as he walked further inside.

"Okay. I'm assuming you were out researching something and not drinking tea in a parlor all morning."

Abner sat in his chair and lit his thinking pipe . He always smoked when he was buried deep in his research. He said it helped him think better, so he'd started calling it his thinking pipe a number of years ago. He opened his briefcase, pulling out a small file as he waved her over.

"I went to the district documents office in Hackney this morning. I found what I believe is your birth records," he said.

"Are you serious?" Spencer dragged her chair over and sat down next to him. "How do you know it's me?"

"Well, I was looking at Mildred Franklin's birth records and timeline. She is surely Abigail Franklin's daughter as the dates and names on the birth certificate match. Before 1900 the records get a little confusing. There weren't birth certificates yet, merely census records and most women of poverty never stayed anywhere long enough to be claimed on a census record. I did however run across a single census from 1892 in the Hackney district." He slid a piece of paper towards her with a section highlighted.

"Is this it?" Spencer asked.

"Yes. An Abigail B. approximate mid thirties in age was a boarder in a hostel during the time this census was taken. She had a female child with her that was approximately three years of age. As you can see the child's name is illegible. This document was rather old obviously and some of it has smeared and withered over the years. If you look real close with the magnifying glass you can make out the first letter of the child's name is an A, but I couldn't make out any other letters."

"Okay, so it's possible this is Abigail Bigsby and her daughter Abigail Franklin. What about Mildred? What was on her birth certificate?"

"Her mother's name and birth date on the certificate coincide with this census. Abigail Franklin was born in November 1888 in Hackney. There is no father listed for Mildred on the birth certificate, which is why she carried on the Franklin last name," he said taking a puff of his pipe.

"So Abigail was thirty-one and a prostitute when she gave birth to Mildred."

"Yes," he ruffled a few papers and set another page from the file in front of her. "Abigail Franklin was thirty-one at the time of her daughter Mildred's birth and Mildred was twenty-four at the time of her daughter Evelyn's birth. If Evelyn was born in 1941 then she was twenty-nine when she gave birth to you."

"Okay."

"There is something else. There was only a single female child born to each woman and each woman was single or at least there was never a father's name listed anywhere."

"Weird," Spencer said.

"Mildred died in 1966. Her death records are in that file there. She died of heart disease probably from living her life in poverty with no healthcare and malnutrition on top of it. I'm sorry to tell you Evelyn passed away as well. Her death certificate is dated five years ago. She died of pneumonia during the winter of 2008. She probably walked the streets until her death and died as a result of that."

"Wow. I'm...I don't know what to say. Their stories are so heartbreaking. I don't understand how I came from that family and turned out the way I did."

"Your adoptive parents saved you."

"Yes. Yes, they did. I only wish I could tell them how thankful I am. They passed away ten years ago in a car accident," she said sadly.

"I'm sorry," Abner replied.

Spencer smiled and patted his hand. "Thank you. They were amazing parents to me and obviously a godsend."

Abner took the papers in front of Spencer and slid them neatly into the file, before pulling out another two pages and placing them on the desk.

"What's this?" she asked.

"Your birth certificate."

"What?" She began to exam the copied document. "Are you sure this is me?"

"Carlene Porter was born to Evelyn Porter in 1980. The hospital records indicate the child was given to an agency in London that adopted children all over Britain and Ireland. When I researched the agency, I learned that it closed some twenty years ago and all of the records were unfortunately destroyed."

"How will I ever know if that is my bloodline since Evelyn has passed away?"

"Well, you could have her exhumed and run her DNA against yours."

Spencer cringed. "I think that's going a little further than I'd like to go."

"Or you can try to find your twin brother," he added.

"What are talking about?"

Abner moved the pages around to reveal the second page. It was another birth certificate identical to hers with the same date and mother's name and the time of birth was five minutes after hers to the exact second.

"Collin Porter," Spencer said.

"Yes. He is your twin brother."

"Oh my God," Spencer exclaimed. "Tell me you found him, Abner."

"Not yet. He seemed to drop off out of the records a few years ago. He was adopted at the same time you were and he wound up with a family that lived close to Wimbledon."

"We have to find him."

"Didn't you have a theory you wanted to run by me?" he asked.

"That can wait."

Abner smiled and put his pipe back in the holder.

"His adoptive parents are both still alive and I have their address. Maybe they can tell us where he is. They may even know more about Evelyn."

Spencer ran through the pouring rain and slid down into the front seat of the tiny two door canary yellow car parked by the curb. She was sure it was smaller than a Smart Car and it was electric.

"Is this thing safe?" she asked.

"Of course it is. I've had this car ten years now and it's nearly as old as you are. You won't find a single scratch on it," Abner replied, checking his mirror for traffic before pulling away.

"How often do you drive this thing?"

"Oh a couple times a year I go up to the countryside for a picnic in the Peak District and see a show or shop the little stores in Nottingham. I have a dear old friend that lives in the Sheffield area of Yorkshire."

"That sounds nice. The only time I get out of the city is when a case takes me away. I don't even own a car anymore. My parents lived upstate so that's where I grew up and since they've been gone I haven't had a reason to return to the area I guess."

"I used to take the train everywhere and one day I decided I wanted to take my time and see the sights when I travel. I used to travel more often when I was younger. Benji, my friend in Yorkshire, he isn't an admirer of London. Therefore, I travel to see him mostly. We traveled to Ireland on holiday a few years back and had a wonderful time. I do believe it's quite beautiful and so green."

"What cities were you in?"

"We started in Dublin, but traveled all over, staying at small bed and breakfasts along the way. We stayed over longer than planned. Where did you live?"

"My parents and I lived in Balbriggan. It's a small town on the northeastern coast above Dublin. My father sold his textile business and we moved to the States when I was in grade school."

"Did you ever travel back to see other family?"

"No, not often. My parents were actually from Drogheda, so we went there a few times to visit people, but I was never fully welcomed into the family. Everyone knew I was an English child. They all had red hair and freckles." she grinned. "I stood out worse than a half-breed."

"That's disgraceful."

"Yes, it was. My parents didn't want me to be teased all of my life and they refused to move to England, so they followed the American dream. Of course, I fit right into the hodgepodge of the States," she laughed.

Abner pulled the car up to the curb in front of a small white house and shut the engine off. They had left the pouring rain behind in London.

"This is it. Their names are Kenneth and Barbara Rolands. They kept Collin's birth name from what I saw in his records."

"Here we go," Spencer said, walking up to the door. She knocked and took a step back next to Abner. A man with thick white hair opened the door.

"Hello, Mr. Rolands, I presume?"

"Yes," the man replied.

"I am Dr. Abner Montague and this is Spencer Donovan. We would like to ask you a few questions about your son Collin and possibly speak with him if you know where we may locate him."

The man gave Abner a strange look and glanced at Spencer.

"Who is it, dear?" a woman called from inside.

"Some people here asking about Collin," he answered. "Who are you with and why are you inquiring about my son?"

"I'm a historian and a professor of history at the London University and this is my colleague from the United States. We've run across some documents that may possibly pertain to Collin Rolands and we are unable to locate him," Abner said.

"I'm not sure what you are talking about, but Collin died nearly three years ago," the man exclaimed.

"Oh my, pardon our intrusion. We were unaware of his passing."

"Well, come in anyway, I guess. Maybe my wife and I can answer your questions."

Spencer led the way as the man waved them inside the small house. A slender woman with grayish brown hair walked out of the kitchen, wiping her hands on the apron around her waist.

"Hello, would either of you care for a spot of tea?" she asked.

"I would love one," Abner said.

"No, thank you," Spencer replied.

"Please, come into the parlor and have a seat. I'm Kenneth Rolands and this is my wife Barbara. "

"It's nice to meet you both. I'm sorry we are meeting under these circumstances." Abner took the cup of tea offered to him. "Thank you."

"What would you like to know about our son?" Barbara questioned, sitting in the chair across from them and next to her husband.

"I'm a historian and I was doing a bit of research that led me to Collin's name. Did either of you happen to know anything about his birth mother or family?"

"No, nothing. The adoption agency just said she was from London's East End and had been unable to care for him," Barbara answered.

"I believe I ran across his mother, grandmother, and great-grandmother in my research. I wanted to see if they had ever tried to contact him and possibly run a DNA test to see if he is truly part of that bloodline," Abner added, sipping his tea.

"Were they royalty or something?" Kenneth asked.

Abner smiled, shaking his head. "No, sir. They were actually ladies of the night with a bloodline possibly dating back to the 1800's and may have had a connection to the Jack the Ripper story."

"Oh wow, that's interesting. Is his birth mother alive?"

"I'm afraid she passed away some five years ago I believe."

"So you're saying his birth mother was a whore?"

"Yes, sir. She, her mother, and her grandmother were all ladies of the night."

"And he was possibly related to Jack the Ripper, you think?"

"It's a theory that his great-grandmother was Jack's illegitimate child. The Jack the Ripper case is all over

51

London history books and often comes up in lectures. Being unsolved has made it a very wide open topic that is still investigated by hundreds of people every year."

"Is that why you are here?" Kenneth turned to Spencer.

"Yes, part of it."

"Well, I'm sorry I can't help either of you with your research. Collin passed away in a tragic accident in Dublin, Ireland. He was cremated and his ashes were spread around Buckingham Palace. He always said his bloodline was royalty and one day he would prove it."

"So, he knew he was adopted?"

"Oh yes, we told him when he was about ten or twelve. It had always bothered him that he didn't have any siblings. One day, I guess he was maybe eight, he came home from school and began talking about a new friend he'd made and how this young boy also had no siblings. He later found out the boy was adopted and began asking us questions, so we told him the truth. Ever since that day he swore he was royal blood," Barbara said with a smile.

"We should probably get going. Thank you both for speaking to us. Again our condolences on your son's passing," Abner exclaimed.

Chapter Seven

Abner drove in silence and Spencer sat quietly in the passenger seat watching the buildings go by. It took a bit longer to go back through town this late in the day, but they soon arrived in front of Abner's brownstone building.

"I need to drive over a block to put the car away. I'll be back in a few minutes," he said dropping her off at the curb with the keys to the office and the flat.

Spencer was sitting at her desk typing notes on her laptop when Abner returned.

"The rain is threatening the skies again," he implied, taking off his Derby hat and overcoat before sitting down in his desk chair. "So, you didn't say much on the way back. I'm sorry about your brother."

"It's okay. I didn't know him anyway. I guess that's a dead end to my family tree then. You researched it all the way to him and I."

"Yes, I do believe that is the end. This morning you mentioned a theory. What was it?"

"Mary Kelly, she's the last of the canonical five. I know the Whitehall Mystery is next in the timeline, but we will get back to that later," Spencer muttered, shuffling the notes in her file.

Abner unfolded the map with the colored circles. Spreading it across his desk, he placed his finger on the red circle indicating the site of Mary Kelly's murder.

"Mary was young, much younger than all of the others. Some twenty years younger in most cases. She was also pretty and was known to have a lot of attractions." Spencer walked over to Abner's desk with her notes.

"Why do you think he chose her?" Abner asked.

"I think she reminded him of Abigail Bigsby. Remember he was unable to find her because she had disappeared. I think he saw Mary Kelly on the street or even in the Ten Bells Pub where most of the girls hung around. He saw her and was reminded of his hatred and anger."

Abner leaned back in his squeaky chair, once again puffing his pipe.

"We've come back to the letter once again," he added. "But, I do believe you may have a very good theory here. Something fueled him the night he murdered Mary Kelly. That something could very well be the reasons he chose her and mutilated her the way he did. Why did she bring him home though? She'd never brought anyone home with her."

"He followed her in the shadows until they were close to her residence. When he stepped into the light, he probably showed interest and they were already near the area, so she took him inside with her. He let her undress down to a chemise or undergarment and he dove on top of her. This is why she was turned to the right, you see she was trying to get away from him when he lunged, but it was too late. She had no time to scream as he sliced her throat through to the vertebrae in the back of her neck, rendering her silent. When she was immobile he went to work, cutting her face beyond recognition and completely opening her chest and abdominal cavities. I'm not sure why he removed so many of her organs, placing them all around the bed. He was in a fit of rage and more than likely had gone black in the mind. I honestly don't think it was ritualistic. It was almost like he wanted her open for the world to see what she was like on the inside. That's why he skinned her like an animal."

"What do you think about the placement of the organs?" Abner asked.

"Her heart was removed, making her body heartless and her uterus, one breast, and kidneys were placed under her head simply to hide them. I believe he didn't want to see her uterus. The liver was placed between the feet with the other breast next to the right foot. The intestines were along one side and the spleen on the other side. It's so random I'm not sure of the reasoning behind this, other than that's just where he put them. Probably because it was open space on the small bed. He stacked all of the skin and tissue on the night table next to the bed in the beginning, which gave him more room to spread her organs all about. How he did all of this without getting enough blood on himself to leave a trail behind is beyond me. He took his time, maybe two or more hours. The timeline is a bit conflicting and she wasn't found until after ten a.m. the following morning."

"The scene of the crime and literal mutilation is proof this was a viscous fit of rage, yet the murderer was calm, collected, and careful not to track evidence or make any suspicious noise."

"Yes, I agree. It's as if he was on autopilot," Spencer said. "He was so distraught over Abigail's abortion that he was driven over the edge of sanity. It's rather sad if you ask me."

"It's also fairly clear he stopped when he found out it was all a lie. It's very possible his mind set right and he went back to living a normal life," Abner stated.

"Oh yes, that is very true. The other Whitechapel murders were not him. There was reasoning behind his killing. The other's were all random acts and more than likely done by different people."

"Many have said he committed suicide, that is why the murders stopped," Abner added, puffing his pipe. Spencer watched the sweet cherry scented smoke swirl around his head.

"That could be very true as well. He learned of his daughter and saw her for the first time just after Mary Kelly's murder. Maybe he felt some regret or even grief over what he had done to all of the women. Here is where that theory may be incorrect, based on the story your great-grandfather and grandfather passed down he was alive in 1912 when Mildred his granddaughter was born. He would have been in his fifties or sixties by then and probably didn't live much past 1914. If in fact that was him that your grandfather saw in the office. It was some twenty years after the murders though, which would mean he didn't commit suicide right away as speculated. Of course, this is if we go by the letter and of course the story passed down in your family."

"Ah, yes that is true. My grandfather told me of the story himself when I was a boy and it was later repeated by my father when he allowed me to care for the letter and begin my own research. One thing is for certain, no matter when he died, we do know that he did stop and because of that letter we have a pretty good reason as to what drove him to do what he did and what caused him to end his reign of terror."

"I wonder if he knew his daughter was a whore just as her mother was?" Spencer asked.

"We have no way of knowing and since he more than likely passed away sometime in 1914 or not long after, he never knew his granddaughter and great-granddaughter were ladies of the night either."

"Here is the big question, how do we take all of that and apply it to the ghost of a man wreaking havoc on London now?" Spencer said.

"That is where you come in, Ms. Donovan. You've already opened my eyes to a whole new theory on Jack the Ripper, that is truer than any other I have run across in my forty years of researching JTR, and the theories that have derived over time."

Spencer walked back to her desk and grabbed another file.

"In order to catch his ghost I knew I had to get into his head. Now that I've accomplished that, we need to figure out what is driving this new ghost of a killer." Spencer took the new file over to Abner's desk and opened it. "Do you know any police detectives, preferably the one in charge of this case?"

"I do know of a few detectives, yes."

"Wonderful, we need to set up a meeting, today if possible."

"I will see what I can do. They may not be willing to show you their evidence straightaway. You're an American, remember?" He smiled.

"Yes, well tell them I'm an Irish lassie born in London's East End and I come here by way of America. That should get their attention." She grinned.

~

Spencer went to work reading local newspapers online and collecting as much information as she could on the new murders, while Abner made phone call after phone call trying to get someone working on the current case to agree to meet with them.

Just before dark, Abner slammed the phone down and pushed back away from his desk.

"We have a meeting before dawn tomorrow with Detective Inspector Shane Thompson. He's a fair man, easy to get along with most of the time. He called me into a meeting a few years back for my expertise on stolen historical artifacts."

"Thompson. Is he Irish?" Spencer asked.

"Why yes, he is." Abner nodded with a grin.

Chapter Eight

Detective Inspector Thompson arrived at Abner's office just before dawn as promised. As the doorbell rang, Abner grabbed Spencer's arm at the bottom of the staircase.

"We mustn't speak of the letter. If Scotland Yard ever finds out about the letter it would taint my family name and you would be tormented by press. Not to mention the letter would be archived and you and I would never see it again," he said to her.

"I completely agree. I wasn't going to bring up any of my theories on JTR, just the profile that I've built based on the old evidence that I've seen."

Abner nodded and walked over to the door.

"It's good to see you again, Inspector Thompson," Abner said pulling the door open.

"Dr. Montague." He nodded, removing his gentlemen's hat. He was wearing a dark suit and tie and was fair skinned with reddish blond hair and thin matching mustache. Spencer noticed he was at least half a foot taller than Abner when he stood next to him.

"This is the woman I spoke to you about," Abner mentioned, waving in Spencer's direction.

"Hello Inspector, I'm Spencer Donovan," she added shaking his hand.

"What exactly has brought you all the way to London from America?" he asked.

"Well, Dr. Montague was doing some research for me about my family. You see, I was born in London, adopted and raised in Ireland, then my family moved to America when I was a child."

"I see. Why has our new murderer interested you so?" he said.

"In the States I am a Criminal Prosecutor and I am a former Criminologist for the FBI, so my background is all about forensic investigation. I guess you can say it's my forte, so to speak." She shrugged. "I heard in the news about the murder a few weeks ago and then of course the one a few days ago. When Dr. Montague mentioned that they were in locations nearly the same as Jack the Ripper I began looking into the Whitechapel murders in 1888 and 1889. I believe you may have a copycat killer on your hands or being how this is the 125th anniversary of those murders, perhaps a ghost. I am here to offer my expertise and possibly help you stop a mad man."

Inspector Thompson looked from Spencer to Abner and back again, still holding his hat in his hand and standing firmly in the center of the room.

"A ghost you say?"

Spencer shrugged. "Possibly."

"What exactly is it that you think you can help me with?"

"I've come up with a profile of Jack the Ripper. If in fact your killer is a copycat, I may be able to use that profile to dictate his next move. Thus, giving you a chance to apprehend him," she replied.

"And if it's a ghost?" he asked with a laugh.

"I am not a Ghost Buster, so I'd suggest you contact someone who is."

"And if it is a true copycat, how exactly will you be able to prove that and the fact that he is following the same profile?"

"I will need to take a look at your evidence and autopsy reports on the victims."

Inspector Thompson sneered. "I think not. That is absurd. Why would I trust some American lawyer with the evidence of a case such as this?"

"What if that American lawyer can help you solve the case? Isn't it your job to catch the killer at all costs? Or was the Prime Minister lying when he said the inspectors are working diligently around the clock and will pull out all the stops to catch this murderer or these murderers however it may be," Abner stated.

"I'm sorry, Dr. Montague, this is just way out of the realm of the way Scotland Yard investigates a case."

"Maybe that's why it has been so easy for him to come back," Spencer declared, turning her back to walk away. She turned around at the bottom of the staircase. "Inspector, on September eighth, just shy of three days from now, a woman will be murdered and found on Hanbury Street between Brick Lane and Wilkes Street. Her throat will be sliced almost decapitating the body. There will be signs of suffocation as well, and her abdomen will be open with her intestines severed and placed on her shoulders. The uterus and it's attachments will be completely removed and missing from the scene."

"How is that you know all of this? And what makes you think the next victim will be treated in such a manner?" Inspector Thompson asked.

"That is what Jack the Ripper did to his second victim, Annie Chapman. If this is Saucy Jack's ghost, he will follow in the same manner." Turning, she walked up the stairs and into the flat.

"I told you she is a very smart woman, Inspector. Don't be so quick to turn her away," Abner expressed as he opened the door for the inspector to exit.

~

"I'd be willing to bet there are two surviving attack victims, as well as the two murders and he has no idea they are all linked. He will have a rude awakening in a few days," Spencer conveyed to Abner as he walked into the room. She was standing at the window watching the dark car drive away.

"Oh, I do believe you are correct. He will return."

"We have a couple of days. What shall we do?" Abner walked over to the sitting chair and poured a cup of tea. Spencer soon followed, but declined the offered tea.

"You know something, I was thinking about the Franklin women and Evelyn Porter when I woke up this morning. None of their children ever had a father listed. I wonder if it's because they didn't know who the father was or just generally hated men. We know that Jack was the father of Abigail, but there wasn't really a birth certificate back then, so we really have no idea and Franklin was her mother's name."

"Yes. There are a lot of strange occurrences in that bloodline. The women were all young, unmarried prostitutes, and they all gave birth to girls, until Evelyn had you and Collin. He is the first boy in the line."

"I wonder if any of the women had other children?" Spencer questioned.

"No, not that I've found. They probably had multiple abortions I'm sure. It was uncommon for a whore to keep a child."

"For some odd reason they all kept one at least long enough to birth it."

"I'd like to find out where Evelyn Porter, Mildred Franklin, and Abigail Franklin are all buried."

"I have it listed in my files. Ironically, they are all buried in the City of London Cemetery, which is where three of Jack's victims were also buried: Mary Nichols, Annie Chapman, and Catherine Eddowes were all buried there at one time. Annie Chapman has since been buried over, but Catherine and Mary have plaques over their burial sites."

"What about the other two?"

"Mary Kelly was buried in St. Patrick's Roman Catholic Cemetery and Elizabeth Stride was buried in the East London Cemetery."

"Is there a florist near there?"

"Yes, at least there is one on the way."

"Good, I'd like to go pay my respects to these women whose lives we have picked apart in the past few days."

"That sounds like a splendid idea. I'll fetch the car," Abner chimed, putting on his dark brown overcoat and matching Derby hat before leaving in a hurry.

The tiny electric car pulled up next to the curb and Abner beeped the horn. Spencer locked the door to the office and slid into the front seat.

"How far are we going?" she asked.

"Not too far. There is a florist right up the street here," he said, pulling away from the curb into the traffic.

"Is this thing charged up and ready to go?"

Abner raised his chin and shook his head. "Electric cars are as common here as pickups in the States. I assure you, we won't have any problems."

"I'm just checking," she replied with a laugh.

"What's so funny?"

"I'm trying to picture you driving a big four-wheel drive pickup," she snickered.

Abner turned the car down a side street which came out onto another street full of traffic and maneuvered the car to the curb.

"This is the only florist I know of in the area. Mrs. Kingsley owns the shop. You will need seven flowers. She probably has some small premade of arrangements if you want that instead of individual flowers," Abner stated.

"You're not coming in?" Spencer asked.

"No. I'm going to plug the car in and make a quick phone call."

Spencer laughed and got out. She returned a few minutes later with seven yellow roses. Abner had already unplugged the car and was sitting patiently waiting for her.

"Those are nice," he said as he started the car.

"She only had three premade arrangements and I like these better anyway."

They drove the rest of the short distance in silence. When they reached the gates, Abner pulled through and stopped at the front to grab a map indicating the plot numbers. He handed the map and a piece of paper to Spencer.

"Those are the plot numbers for everyone. Look them up on the map. There are close to a million people buried here."

"Wow. Okay." Spencer began searching the map drawing a circle around each plot number as she found it. She directed Abner towards the plot nearest to them.

"This is where Mary Nichols is buried," she said as they got out of the car.

Spencer and Abner walked up to the bronze plaque that had Mary's name, birth date, and date of death stenciled on it. They stood together quietly in a moment of silence and Spencer placed a yellow rose next to the plaque before walking away. They repeated the same steps for the other two Ripper victims before journeying to the other side of the cemetery where her family members were scattered.

Abigail Franklin had a tiny rock posing as a headstone with her name and birth and death dates. Mildred Franklin had much of the same thing. Spencer silently placed roses next to the rocks. Evelyn Porters death was more recent causing a slightly larger headstone to be erected over her grave. It still wasn't as large or as fancy as most of the other stones in the lot, but it had her name and dates etched in the stone.

"I'm not sure if I would've wanted to know her," Spencer said to Abner. She wiped a lone tear from her cheek and knelt down, placing her wet hand on the cold stone over Evelyn's name. She paused for a moment of silence and placed the last yellow rose from her hand next to the stone before standing up.

"I hope they are all resting peacefully," Spencer whispered, sliding into the car.

8 SEPTEMBER 2013

He walked along the dimly lit sidewalk in silence choosing to stop and wait at a darkened corner. Five minutes had barely come and gone when Beverly Coleman sashayed in front of him wearing a short skirt with her blouse tied high around her waist. The streets were silent. It had been nearly twenty minutes since the last car passed by. He waited until she was a few feet away before stepping from the shadows.

He cleared his throat and grinned when the startled woman turned around.

"You scared me," she said and smiled. "Are you looking for some company?"

He nodded. "I have a car nearby," he said. He had a very guttural sounding voice.

She hesitated for a second then grinned. "Show me the way."

He walked half a block and turned down a side street where a dark car was parked by the curb. He waved her around to the passenger side as he climbed in behind the wheel. As soon as she shut her door he grabbed her tightly, placing a wet rag over her face before she could scream. Her body went limp in his arms and he pushed her to the side. He quickly checked the streets for signs of movement before starting the car and driving away.

She woke up on the cold cement floor in a small room. A soft light was glowing in the corner casting shadows on the wall. She felt something tied tight around her neck and reached up to touch it. Her stepped over her so quickly she never saw the knife coming as it sliced through her neck just below the ribbon of the handkerchief and down to the vertebrae of her spine. Blood poured from her carotid artery, pooling on the floor under her. He wiped the knife on her clothing and moved to the side of her, spreading her legs apart.

He sliced her abdomen down to her pelvis laying her open like a dissected animal in science class. Then, he pushed her bowels and other organs to the side revealing her uterus and bladder. He made swift delicate cuts, avoiding the rectum and dividing the vagina as he cut the uterus and it's appendages loose and placed them on the floor next to her body. He closed the flaps of her abdomen and covered the area with a thick saddle blanket as he carried her outside. He stuffed her body into the trunk of the car and went back inside.

The large stone fireplace was lit and roaring with orange flames in the room adjacent to the cold cement room where he kept the old steamer trunk with his knives. He wrapped the bloody organs laying on the floor in newspaper and tossed them in the fire across the hall. He waited, watching it shrivel and pop like bacon as it burned. When there was nothing but ashes left on the casually flaming pieces of wood he extinguished the remaining fire with a bucket of water and went back outside to the car.

He drove slowly through the darkened streets towards Hanbury Street. Satisfied that no other cars were around he parked at the curb and pulled her body out of the trunk tossing the blanket back inside. He positioned her body with her knees bent, her feet close together, and her legs spread apart. He opened the flap of her abdomen. Quickly severing her intestines, he placed them around her shoulders and moved her left arm across her breasts. He left her blue eyes wide open, watching him as he walked back to the car and drove away.

Chapter Nine

Abner was sitting in a chair across from Spencer in the flat. The sun had yet to rise and he was already enjoying his morning cup of tea. Spencer was sipping the nastiest cup of instant coffee imaginable, but it was better than tea in her opinion. She was returning emails on her phone and writing a new email on her laptop to her assistant explaining that it was taking a lot longer than expected and she was unsure when she would be returning home. Her position with the State would be in jeopardy soon and she would need to make a decision.

The doorbell down below buzzed, causing both of them to jump, then harsh pounding on the door instantly grabbed their attention. Abner checked the pocket watch he kept in his vest pocket.

"Who would be calling on me at this hour?" he questioned, walking towards the staircase. Spencer picked up her laptop and followed him, waiting at the bottom to see who was pounding the door and ringing the bell over and over.

Abner pulled the door open and stepped aside as Inspector Thompson pushed his way inside.

"I beg your pardon," Abner said to him.

"You," Inspector Thompson pointed at Spencer. "Tell me how it is that you know the details to last night's carnage, before I arrest you here on the spot!" he yelled.

"Whoa, calm down," she exclaimed, setting her laptop on the bookshelf.

"I presume another woman has been found?" Abner implied, closing the door.

"Yes. And it is just as she said it would be. I want to know how you knew of it, Ms. Donovan."

Spencer walked over to her desk. Opening the thick file, she spread it out in front of him.

"Do you see this?" She pointed at the old grainy black and white picture of a woman's body. "This is Annie Chapman. September 8th, 1888, Jack the Ripper cut her throat, opened her abdomen removing her uterus and he spread her intestines over her shoulder. He did all of this on Hanbury Street. Read the investigation if you don't believe. I told you, Inspector, you either have Saucy Jack's ghost or one hell of a copycat killer on your hands. I assure you, I am not either one." She crossed her arms. "I am here to help you. If you would just let me."

"I can attest to her alibi she was here all evening. We stayed up playing cards until after midnight and she slept upstairs on the couch in my flat all night," Abner stated.

"This is evidence, all of it," Inspector Thompson said, pointing to the files on the desk.

"This is no such thing," Abner retorted. "These files are my research and property of London University."

Spencer sighed, rolling her eyes. "Inspector Thompson, do you know what the Internet is?"

"Yes, of course."

"Do you know how to *use* the Internet?"

"What do you take me for?" he sneered.

"At the moment, I probably shouldn't answer that question," Spencer replied, walking over to her laptop sitting on the side of the bookcase. She placed it on her desk and typed the word: *Ripperologist* into the search box. Over a hundred websites popped up and she clicked on the first one. Over a thousand pages of information on Jack the Ripper were on the site including the letters, investigations, and pictures of the victims.

"This information is accessible to anyone with a computer, Inspector. Millions of people probably have copies of your *evidence*," she said sarcastically.

Inspector Thompson sat down in her chair, placing his hat next to the laptop on the desk in front of him. He stared at the screen for a moment sighing as he rubbed his finger back and forth over his moustache.

"I'm afraid I know none of the Ripper story. I am at a great disadvantage," Inspector Thompson conveyed quietly.

"I know the story. Quite well actually," Spencer said.

"Do you know how to stop him?" he asked without looking away from the screen.

"I believe so," she answered.

"No one can know about this. Any of this," he stated harshly. Showing his defeat he sighed once more looking up at her. "What do you need from me?"

Spencer grabbed a piece of paper and began making a list.

"I need everything you have on all three of your murder victims: names, addresses, employment history. I also need copies of all of your evidence, including autopsy reports and photos, witness testimony, and anything else that pertains to the case."

Spencer made a note at the bottom with a star next to it.

"I also need you to look into your records for possible attack victims on or around February twenty-fifth and March twenty-eighth. They will have been stabbing in the lower torso and or throat. If there are no police reports, check with the hospitals."

Inspector Thompson read the notes before folding the paper and slipping it into his jacket pocket. "How much time do I have?" he asked.

"Roughly three weeks until he strikes again. There is something else you need to know, Inspector."

"What is that?"

"He will kill two women this time."

The blood drained from Inspector Thompson's already pale face as he stood up. He nodded and put his hat back on as he walked towards the door.

"I will be in touch soon." He walked out without looking back.

Spencer watched Abner sitting at his desk filling his pipe.

"I dare say, that was a bit interesting. Don't you agree?" he expressed cheerfully.

"Interesting to say the least." Spencer sat down in her chair and shuffled her papers back into the file folder. "It looks as if I may be staying a lot longer than anticipated."

"Yes. Yes it does. We can move you to a hotel in the city if you'd like. Of course, you're still welcome to use my couch and stay up all hours of the night entertaining an old man with card games." He smiled.

"I'd like to stay here if it's all the same to you. I feel comfortable here," she replied. She wasn't sure why, but she felt like Abner's small flat and tiny office were the safest place to be at the moment.

"End of discussion then," Abner agreed, puffing his pipe.

Spencer picked up her cell phone and pushed a speed dial button. She watched the smoke swirl above Abner's head as she waited on the line.

"Hello," the bubbly voice sounded almost squeaky through the phone.

"Josie, it's Spencer."

"Ms. Donovan, I wasn't expecting you to call after I got your email a bit ago."

"I know. I'm sorry to call you so early, but there has been a huge change in my plans. It seems London may have a serial killer on their hands and I've been asked to put my expertise to use in helping solve this mystery. I'm not sure when I will be returning. I could very well be here another month. I will contact the governor myself later today. He may ask for my resignation, but my hopes are that he will understand and be grateful that my skills are such an asset."

"Oh, wow. Okay, I'll continue to forward your calls to your voicemail and adjust your schedule until I know otherwise."

"Thanks," Spencer replied before hanging up.

"I didn't think your employment would ever be an issue while you were here," Abner said.

"Yes, well I didn't plan to be here more than two days at the most and I've already been here a week. Now, I'm looking at another three weeks at least. The Governor of New York will only let me put my cases aside for so long."

"Maybe Scotland Yard can contact him."

Spencer laughed. "That would be a long shot. Besides, Inspector Thompson said no one is to know about you and I assisting in this investigation. I'm sure he is putting his badge on the line, but at the same time, I'm sure he is being pushed to solve this case quickly before London realizes these murders are linked."

"I believe you're correct. After the fumbling mess they made in 1888 I doubt they don't want that to happen again. I'm still a bit shocked he has agreed to show you everything. You are an American after all." He smiled.

Spencer grinned. "I'm still shocked he wanted to arrest me. I think I may have slapped him if he had tried to handcuff me."

Abner laughed, causing him to choke a little on the pipe smoke.

~

Inspector Thompson knocked on Abner's office door shortly after the lunch hour. He held tightly to the thick file folder he was carrying and moved inside quickly when Abner opened the door.

"This is everything from the three murders. I'm still working on the attacks. So far, there are no reports that I know of, unless the City of London Police were notified. I'm headed to the hospitals now to begin checking their records," he said, placing the file on Spencer's desk.

"The city police wouldn't be involved. At least, not until the next two murders. One of them will take place in Mitre Square. The rest of them were in the Whitechapel

District or at least the jurisdiction of the Metropolitan Police or more formally known, Scotland Yard, at the time."

"Grand," Inspector Thompson said sarcastically.

Spencer walked over to Abner's desk and opened the large map they had been using to plot the murders. She ran her finger over the areas where Ada Wilson and Annie Millwood were attacked.

"I may be able to narrow it down for you, Inspector. Start with Royal London Hospital and Mile End Hospital. Those are in the areas where the two attacks should have occurred. In fact, to narrow it even further, you are looking for a woman that would have been stabbed in the lower torso and legs around February twenty-fifth at Royal London and Mile End you are looking for a woman stabbed in the neck possibly in her home or brothel or wherever she is staying. This should have happened on March twenty-eighth."

"You know you're a bit frightening with this information," Inspector Thompson said. "I'll return when I have information."

Spencer and Abner watched him leave before delving into the file he supplied.

Chapter Ten

Spencer separated the papers and pictures from the new file. There were three victims, Tracy Wright, Delilah Anderson, and Beverly Coleman.

"Here, this may be helpful," Abner said, pulling a large dry erase board out from behind the end of the bookcase. It was at least three feet wide and on wheels. It looked completely out of place in the antiquely decorated room, which is why Abner kept it hidden away when it wasn't in use.

"It's good to see you have partly stepped into the twenty-first century," she teased.

"Yes, well," Abner tweaked his mustache and went back to the file.

Spencer wrote the first woman's name at the top of the board with a line under it. Below that she wrote the attack date and location.

"Tracy Wright was a known prostitute in the King's Cross area, but was possibly working in Victoria the night she was picked up. Two of the witnesses reported speaking to her just after one in the morning. Both women saw a dark car, but only one saw the driver. She said he had dark hair, a dark beard, maybe a mustache too, and was wearing a funny looking hat like a TV mobster would wear. Neither woman was sure Tracy got into the car though. They went around to the next corner."

"He's targeting night workers just as JTR had," Abner said.

Spencer pulled the crime scene report out of the pile of papers and wrote more notes on the board.

"She was found on Gunthorpe Street outside of Sunley House."

"That's in the general location of the old George Yard Buildings where Martha Tabram was found," Abner added, making a new colored circle on the map.

"There was little blood under the body and no trace of blood spatter. There were also no tire tracks as the road is asphalt and the curb yielded no footprints or handprints. She was most definitely not stabbed there. He picked her up in Victoria, killed her somewhere, and dumped her at the Martha Tabram location."

Abner grabbed the autopsy report from the pile.

"She was fifteen days shy of her thirty-eighth birthday, five foot four inches, with a slender build, brown hair and eyes. The time of death is estimated around two a.m. She had a total of thirty-nine stab wounds in the lungs, heart, liver, spleen, and stomach. The general focusing seemed to be on the breasts, belly, and groin areas. All of the wounds except for one were made with a short single-edged blade similar to a pocket knife. The wound to the heart was made with a large object yielding a double-sided blade."

"That report couldn't be any more similar to Martha Tabram's post-mortem report," Spencer remarked. She moved the pages to locate the file folder on the Whitechapel murder's victims. She pulled Martha Tabram's file from the folder and wrote her name at the top of the board next to Tracy Wright's. She then listed all of Martha's murder information just as she had done with Tracy's and stepped back.

"That is uncanny," Abner exclaimed, reading the board.

"Copy all of this down on a piece of paper for Inspector Thompson," Spencer said as she began pulling the papers for the next murder victim from the inspector's file.

Abner quickly finished and she erased the board, writing Delilah Anderson's name at the top with a line under it. She followed the same routine writing her body location and date.

"She was found on Durward Street near Kempton Court," Spencer informed, writing the notes on the board.

"That area was originally called Buck's Row. Mary Nichols' body was found there near the boarding school and cottages across the way," Abner added.

"She was forty-three years old, just over five foot tall, with a petite build. She had brown hair and brown eyes. Her time of death is sometime around two a.m." Spencer handed Abner the autopsy report so she could continue writing.

"Her neck was cut down to the vertebrae severing both arteries. She had several jagged incisions running across her lower torso on both sides and one long deep gash running down her abdomen causing disembowelment." Abner put the paper aside and picked up the investigation report.

"She was last seen on Commercial Street a little after midnight. There were no witnesses when she was picked up. She was probably alone at the time. Her body was found at a quarter after five. There was very little blood found at the scene and no footprints or tire tracks."

"She was dumped. He's obviously killing them somewhere else," Spencer stated. She grabbed the file on Mary Nichols and began writing notes of her murder on the opposite side of the board.

"The similarities are virtually exact," Abner declared, reading the notes on the board.

"It's definitely not a ghost, unless he learned how to drive a car." Spencer grinned.

"I'd have to agree with you on that. He definitely has some sort of transportation and a hidden place that is easily accessible all hours of the night without disturbing the neighbors."

"I'm beginning to think he's not a very big guy, not particularly tall."

"What makes you think that?" Abner asked.

"Look at the two women we've profiled so far. They aren't very tall, less than average height, and they both have a small build. He's choosing women that aren't very big so he can handle them. Think about it. No one heard screams and there are no signs of a struggle. He is able to grab and subdue them easily. He may not be able to do that with a woman say my height five foot six. I'm closer to five foot eight probably with the thick soles and slight heels of my shoes. How tall are you?"

"Five foot five with my shoes on," Abner answered.

Spencer walked around and grabbed him from behind but she couldn't get a grip on his round body.

"See my point? If you were slimmer and a bit shorter I could have held onto you without a struggle," she said.

Abner adjusted his suit jacket and vest. "I agree. So if these women are barely over five feet tall, how tall do you think he is?"

"I'd say he's below six foot, maybe even under five foot ten. My theory could be way off and he's way over six foot and these just happen to be the women he chooses," she added.

"How tall was the last girl?" Abner asked.

"I don't know. I'll get her file together while you copy all of the notes on the board for the inspector."

Spencer wiped the board clean and wrote Beverly Coleman's name at the top left side.

"This is the latest victim. She was found on Hanbury Street near Wilkes Street just before six a.m. According to this report, she hadn't been there long. Her time of death is three a.m. at the latest," Spencer informed as she wrote the notes on the board.

"The autopsy review lists her being forty-one, five foot three, with a small build. She had brown hair dyed blond and hazel eyes."

"She's right in the middle. I think the first woman, Tracy Wright, was the tallest at five foot four."

"I believe she was, yes," Abner agreed before continuing the report.

"Her throat was severed so deeply she was nearly decapitated. She had a handkerchief tied tightly around her neck and her tongue was swollen and slightly protruding indicating possible strangulation. She was more than likely still alive when her throat was cut. Her abdomen was split open down the center and cut across, creating opening flaps. Her uterus and it's extremities were delicately removed so as to avoid cutting the rectum or the cervix. The removed organs were not found at the scene. Her intestines were also severed and found around the victim's shoulders."

"Annie Chapman all over again." Spencer shook her head.

"There was little blood found at the scene so he obviously killed her and removed the uterus at another location. The location is pretty busy so he didn't have much time to dump her. I think the intestines were already removed so all he had to do was put her on the ground and place them around her neck. "

"Where was she picked up?"

"She was well known in Victoria. One woman remembered seeing her before midnight. No one seemed to notice her after that. There was an older woman who had been on her way to church for sunrise service and saw a dark car pull onto Brick Lane from Hanbury. She said it was around four-thirty when she passed by that area and saw the car. She couldn't give a make or model, only it was a dark car."

"How many dark cars are on the streets of London?" Spencer asked.

"Oh hundreds, I'm sure," Abner replied.

"If her TOD is three a.m., then the car is seen at four-thirty, and her body is found at six he must be close by the area. He had to kill her, carefully remove her organs, drive her to the location, and dump her all within an hour and a half if that is in fact his car that was seen. What's the timeframe for Annie's death? Can you check those notes for me please?" Spencer asked.

Abner flipped through the pages until he reached the inquest into Annie Chapman's death.

"She is last seen at five-thirty a.m. talking with a man and her body is found at six a.m."

"Thirty minutes. If Jack the Ripper was able to do what he did there out in the open in less than thirty minutes and disappear then an hour and a half including a short car ride should have been well within reach for our guy. That car could easily have been him leaving the dump scene. It's obvious he has learned some medical skills to be able to repeat these gruesome attacks."

"It is very possible that he either lives close to the area or is using some sort of building in the area."

Spencer nodded in agreement. "I can begin building his profile using the information we have now," she said, moving some of the papers to the side and opening a new document sheet on her laptop.

"I'm going to go make a new pot of tea. Would you care for a cup?" Abner asked.

"No, thank you." Spencer laughed. "I don't know why you still ask," she said shaking her head.

When Abner returned a few minutes later, she went over the profile with him.

"Based on the evidence we have seen so far, he's average height or shorter, with a medium-strong build. He may have dark hair and facial hair. He drives a dark car and has used books or possibly classroom instruction to learn basic anatomy or at least enough to carry out his copied murders successfully. He's targeting prostitutes that are short with small builds. He either lives or kills nearby the Whitechapel District as he is killing in a different location and dumping the bodies. One thing is very certain, he is a Ripperologist or some sort of self-proclaimed Ripper expert. He's studied these cases from every angle maybe even for a number of years. He feels as if he knows JTR. He may even believe he is a reincarnation or something of the sort. He's street smart, but also well educated and very familiar with the Whitechapel murders in general, not just the ones linked to JTR."

~

The next day, Inspector Thompson returned late in the afternoon. Spencer had just gotten off the phone with the Governor of New York, upstairs in the flat.

"Ah, there you are. I was just telling Inspector Thompson of the profile you are building," Abner informed when he saw her at the bottom of the stairs.

"I'd like to take a look at the profile," the inspector said.

"We've also made notes of each new murder and historical murder that it coincides with," Abner replied, handing him the handwritten copies that made.

"I'm afraid I have some bad news," Spencer stated.

"What's wrong?" Abner questioned.

"I need to return to New York tonight for a meeting tomorrow with the Governor. It appears as if I am going to be in the unemployment line by the end of the day if I decide to return here."

"That's absurd!" Abner huffed.

"On what grounds, Ms. Donovan?" Inspector Thompson asked.

"I've been here and away from my job for two weeks now. The New York State justice system isn't going to wait any longer."

"Does this Governor know of your involvement with my investigation?"

"Yes and without proof there is nothing I can do. Even with proof he would probably let me go anyway if I come back here."

"Your services are greatly needed here, Ms. Donovan. I would go to the Prime Minister himself if that would indeed help you."

"Thanks, inspector, but I think I am do for a change anyway. I'm tired of trying the cases of two-bit, lowlife criminals when investigating horrendous crimes and profiling criminals is what I am obviously supposed to be doing. I'll gladly resign and take my severance. I should return in a day or two once I settle my affairs."

"May I ask why you are no longer working for the FBI?"

Abner's ears perked up. He too wanted to know why she left the bureau since he was unable to find out anything about it when he inquired about her.

"Inspector, that's a long story that I simply don't feel like discussing at the moment. Maybe another time," she said solemnly.

Chapter Eleven

Spencer took the red-eye overnight and landed at JFK Airport in New York. She checked her watch and had just enough time to go to her apartment and shower before she had to meet with Governor Cuomo. She was lucky to get a couple hours of sleep on the long eight and half hour flight after typing her resignation. She waved down a taxi and gave him her address.

Walking into the loft apartment, she tossed her suitcase to the side and was greeted by a white and gray Siamese cat making circles and figure eights around her ankles.

"Well, hello there, Alfred. Thank you for not destroying the place while I was gone," Spencer said, bending to pet the reclusive cat. "You're not going to believe this. Jack the Ripper was my great-great-grandfather."

The cat meowed.

"I know unbelievable right." She pet him again before he ran off.

She walked into the kitchen and read the note her friend and cat-sitter had left regarding Alfred's picky appetite.

"You better eat when she feeds you, cat. You're going to starve to death when I leave again," she yelled down the hall in the direction she saw the cat disappear in.

She glanced at the clock on the microwave and ran up the stairs to her office in the loft to grab some case files that she would need to return to the state. She placed them in her briefcase with her ID badge and hurried off to take a quick shower.

~

Spencer arrived for her meeting with the Governor with five minutes to spare. She rushed down the hall of the District Attorney building towards her office.

"Ms. Donovan, I wasn't expecting you." Josie jumped up from her desk.

"Surprise," Spencer said. "The Governor should be here within the next minute or two. I'll call you later to explain everything. Bring him right in when he arrives." Spencer grinned and walked into her office. She opened her laptop and printed her resignation. Then, she placed the file folders that she brought from her home office into the correct filing cabinet.

"Good morning, Governor," Spencer stepped around her desk to shake his hand as soon as he entered her office.

"I hope you used your time wisely on that long flight back to New York," he stated.

"Yes, sir, as a matter of fact I did. I originally went to London because I was summoned by a historian that discovered my natural family. You see, sir, I was adopted and never knew anything about my birth mother or her family. This historian was able to trace my bloodline back a few generations and wanted to share his findings with me in person. A day after my arrival, I was informed of a mysterious murder that had taken place recently. The historian, his name is Dr. Abner Montague, if you care to look him up. Dr. Montague knew of my background and the murder came up in casual conversation. I learned of the second murder while I was awaiting my return flight in the airport. I immediately went back to see Dr. Montague regarding the new murder. A Detective Inspector brought me in as a silent partner on the case after the third body was discovered. I've been going through the case evidence and building a criminal profile for him. I do realize my duties lie first and foremost with the State of New York and the New York City District, but criminology is my passion. Which is why I would like to resign from my position as District Attorney, effective immediately," Spencer said. She slid the sealed envelope containing the typed resignation letter across her desk.

"Are you sure this is what you want to do?" he asked.

"Yes , sir."

"I have no other choice but to accept your resignation. I do wish you well, Spencer. You're a hell of a prosecutor. I hope to see you again someday in the New York State court system, although I'd be happy to recommend you anywhere."

"Thank you. I think I will take a few months off and head back to London to try and catch this killer. After that, I'm not sure what I will do, but I know I want to go back into criminology."

"If it's all the same, you will be missed around here and by the people of New York. I'll call a press conference this evening to announce your resignation. That should give you time to return to London without being hounded. I'm assuming you plan to return today?"

"Yes. My return flight leaves in a few hours," Spencer said.

"It sounds like Scotland Yard might be your next venture. They struck oil when you happened to show up on their doorstep."

She smiled and stood with him, shaking his hand. "I don't have any personal affects, so I'm ready to be escorted from the building."

"Nonsense. You resigned, Spencer. I didn't fire you." He smiled. "Come on, we'll walk out together."

~

Spencer repacked her suitcase, rubbed the top of Alfred's head one last time, and rushed down to the awaiting cab. She called her friend and cat-sitter on the way to the airport to let her know she was heading back to London. She also let her know she left money for Alfred's food and told her to watch the evening news. She wasn't looking forward to another long flight, but she was excited to be returning to the case of a lifetime.

Chapter Twelve

Spencer arrived back in London happy to see Abner's little yellow car waiting by the curb when she stepped outside of Heathrow Airport.

"Aren't you a sight for tired eyes," she said with a smile.

"It's truly awful that you had to resign from your position. I'm sorry my summons has caused you so much grief," Abner replied. He started the car and pulled away from the curb.

"Don't be sorry, Abner. I'm actually grateful for meeting you. You have opened my eyes wider than I ever thought possible. I've learned so much working this case with you and you gave me my real family, albeit they're all deceased. At least I now know who they were and where I come from."

"Shall we stop for one of those dreadful American coffees you love so dearly?"

"That would be wonderful." Spencer watched the buildings pass by as they drove across town. She honestly was happy she returned to London. Going on this journey had opened her eyes to the world around her and she realized she was wasting her life away in a court room when what she really wanted was to be in the middle of the investigation watching it unfold in front of her eyes. She'd missed this kind of excitement.

"I spoke with Inspector Thompson this morning," Abner said.

"What did he have to say?"

"He thinks he may have found our attack victims. He was on the way to take their statements. He said he would be by later with the new information."

"I know they are out there. This guy didn't just start with Tabram. I believe he had practice attacks just as I believe JTR did too."

"I agree. You know we are coming up on the Whitehall murder. Do you think he will imitate that one?"

"No. JTR was his style and he has studied Jack the Ripper enough to know that wasn't one of his murders. If a fresh torso does show up I will be shocked. It would mean he plans on copying all of the Whitechapel murders, not just JTR, or he thinks JTR committed all of them," she replied.

"I still can't believe they haven't found any prints or DNA."

"He's wearing gloves and cleaning the scene thoroughly. He's not trying to get caught. He isn't finished yet. As I said before, he's smart." Spencer unbuckled her seatbelt when Abner parked in a space near the coffee house. "Do you want anything?" she asked.

"Heavens, no," Abner grimaced.

Spencer shrugged and laughed as she walked inside. She returned to the car a few minutes later with a large steaming cup of coffee and a bag full of cream-filled and cheese-filled pastries. Abner's stomach rumbled as he watched her pull a pastry from the bag.

"I thought you didn't want anything." She grinned.

"I didn't know they had those in there."

"These are so much better than your dreadful biscuits." Spencer licked the sugary powder from her lips and took another bite.

Abner huffed and started the car.

"Oh for crying out loud, Abner. Have a damn pastry." She handed him the bag.

"I'm driving at the moment."

Spencer laughed.

"What's so funny?"

"You. You remind me of those old men in the British murder books from years ago. Do you happen to know who Hercule Poirot is?"

"Why yes, of course. Agatha Christie is one of my favorite authors."

"You remind me of him."

"How so?"

"Have you looked in the mirror lately? Your three piece suits, derby hats, pocket watches, handlebar mustache, is any of this ringing a bell?"

"You're turning back into a snooty American," he said, parking the car next to the curb in front of the large brown building where his office and flat were located. "Try not to eat all of the pastries before I return."

Spencer got out of the car and watch him drive away. She wasn't exactly sure where he kept his little electric car parked, but it must have been some garage area with a power box. She was surprised to see how many people plugged their cars in when they stopped at stores. Apparently, many people were driving electric cars.

In all the haste to boot the selfish American out of the car, Abner had forgotten to give her the keys. Spencer was leaning against the office door eating what had to have been her second or third pastry.

"I'm terribly sorry you had to wait for my return." Abner hurried to the door.

"It's fine, just gave me more time to eat another pastry."

Abner waved her inside once the door was unlocked. He took off his overcoat and hat, placing them neatly on the coat rack. He was surprised to see the pastry bag sitting on his desk as he turned around.

"Take your pick. I think there are three left. In fact, you can have them all if you want. I'm full." Spencer placed her briefcase next to her desk and took her suitcase up to the flat. She smiled halfway up when she finally heard the paper bag crinkle.

~

The day was already halfway over by the time Spencer arrived in London and darkness quickly followed as the rest of the day passed. She was engrossed in her notes when the doorbell buzzed, causing her to jump from her seat.

"I'll get it." Abner moved to answer the door.

"Dr. Montague, it's Inspector Thompson." He pounded loudly.

"Come in. Come in," Abner said, pulling the door open.

"Welcome back, Ms. Donovan." Inspector Thompson nodded, removing his hat.

"Thank you. I hear you may have found our attack victims."

"Indeed I have," he acknowledged, handing her a folder. "These are their statements. It took me most of the day to track the second girl. They're both prostitutes I'm afraid."

"I expected that," Spencer said. "All of the victims will be prostitutes. Maybe it's time to heed a little warning to the ladies in the streets. After all, there is a mad man on the loose in the city."

"If we go and tell anyone we have a man ripping up prostitutes on the streets of London, this city would be in an uproar. So far, we've managed to keep most of the details from the press. They've been unable to link the murders on their own."

"Perhaps a very quiet warning, then," Abner implied.

"What do you mean by that?"

"Only tell the ladies of the night. They're the ones in danger anyway."

"I see your point, but I cannot agree. Not at the present time at least," Inspector Thompson said.

"Would it be possible to speak with these two women?" Spencer asked, still holding the folder.

"Take a look at their statements and if it is still warranted, I may be able to get them to talk to you. I shall return in the morning."

Inspector Thompson left and Spencer opened the folder. There were two packets of papers neatly stacked with paperclips in the top corners of each one.

"Cindy Smith and Sheryl Smith, no relation of course," Spencer laughed at the obviously fake names the women chose to use.

"You didn't expect them to use their real names did you?" Abner said.

"Well, no I guess not." Spencer grabbed the first packet, removing the paperclip. "Here, you read this off while I write it on the board," she exclaimed.

"Cindy Smith checked into Royal London Hospital with lower torso and leg stab wounds at three a.m. on the twenty-fifth of February. She was seen by Dr. Schmidt and released around six a.m. The count was inaccurate, but somewhere between six and eight total. None were life-threatening. She received twenty stitches total to close the worst wounds and sent home."

"What does the interview report say?" Spencer asked.

"She was found at a brothel in Victoria after an extensive search all over the city. In her statement she said it was just after one a.m. when a dark car pulled up to her at the curb. She got in and the next thing she knew she woke up bleeding with pain in her lower stomach and upper legs. She used a nearby payphone to call for a cab to take her to the hospital. She also said it was very dark inside the car because it didn't have any interior lights. She could barely tell the man was even sitting next to her. She thinks he had a hat on though."

"Did he speak to her at all?"

"Yes. She said he wanted her to tell everyone he was back."

"That's eerie, but this definitely sounds like our guy," Spencer said.

"Sounds like Annie Millwood too," Abner stated.

"Yes, very much so. Same wounds, similar hospital, prostitute, I believe this was his first victim."

"We're dealing with someone who is very intelligent, but also unstable. Remember he may believe he is a reincarnation or something of the sort. What about the other girl?"

Abner grabbed the other packet. "Sheryl Smith sounds a lot like Ada Wilson. She reportedly checked-in at Mile End Hospital with a stab wound in the throat on March twenty-eighth. The hospital report says it wasn't very deep and missed her arteries. She received five stitches to close it and antibiotics. "

"What did she say to the inspector?"

"He found her near Commercial Street. She said she was staying at a brothel during that time and taking her customers in her room as appointments through phone calls from a payphone card. She thought she was finished for the night when a man knocked on her door. She let him in and he quickly grabbed her from behind and stabbed her. She was in shock and unable to scream. He threw her to the floor and left the room. She said he was wearing dark clothes, a dark hat, and was scruffy looking. She wasn't sure if it was dirt or facial hair."

"Any remarks on his height or hers?"

"No."

"We need to see this girl."

"Yes. I agree."

"They could both know a lot more than they think. Does Scotland Yard have a sketch artist?"

"I'm not sure."

"Get some sleep tonight, Abner. We are going to have a long day tomorrow. We only have six more days."

Chapter Thirteen

Spencer was sitting at her desk in the office when Abner walked down the stairs.

"You're up early," he said.

"Your couch is about as comfortable as a prison cot. Besides, I wanted to get a head start. I've been working on a list of questions to ask the girls, although I'm sure instinct will kick in and I won't even need the list. It's still best to have it anyway, so I don't overlook anything. This may be the one and only time we get to speak to them."

"Inspector Thompson should be here soon. He's notorious for beginning his day above the sunrise."

The doorbell rang and a swift knock followed as soon as Abner sat down in his chair.

"I'll get it," Spencer announced, already rising from her seat.

"I hope you have some information for me," Inspector Thompson said. Removing his hat as he walked inside and turned back towards Spencer.

"Not much, I'm afraid. These attacks are near carbon copies of two Whitechapel murder victims from 1888.

Neither of which was ever considered to be a Jack the Ripper victim. There are theories that speculate that both women were in fact attacked by JTR before he progressed to killing. There is a five month window between Ada Wilson and Martha Tabram who is the first murder victim, but again she is not part of the canonical five as Jack's victim's are referred to as."

"So you're saying our guy did or did not attack these two women?"

"Yes. I'd bet my life these were his first two victims and I'm willing to go out on a limb and say they know more than they're telling you too."

"What makes you say that?"

"Certain details are missing. If you take me to see them I may be able to get the details out of them," Spencer replied.

Inspector Thompson sighed. "It was difficult enough for me to find them the first time."

"Tell them we can meet them wherever they feel comfortable. Prostitution is legal it's not like they are hiding some grand scheme. If they would feel more comfortable I'll talk to them alone. It doesn't matter to me."

"Alright, give me a few hours," Inspector Thompson said. He put his hat back on in such a haste, Spencer thought it looked backwards as he left the office.

"You mentioned that five month window between victims. I know you have a theory here," Abner said.

"Yes. Yes I do." Spencer sat down behind her desk. "How did he go from stabbing to slicing and dicing in five months? I believe it is during these five months that JTR perfected his plan and honed his skills by either reading books on the anatomy and or possibly working in a mortuary or a crematorium which is even better. No one would notice him hacking up bodies because they were cremated."

"His letter mentions he wasn't a doctor, so I'm pretty certain that is out of the question," Abner stated.

"Exactly. I do believe our ghost may have spent the five months in a similar fashion especially since he already had specific instructions for each victim thanks to the Ripperologist websites. He spent the time perfecting his work so that he could make it as identical as possible."

"Do you think he works or has worked in the medical field?"

"No. I doubt it. His access to bodies is much more limited than Jack's was. That's why he takes them away to another location. He isn't skilled enough to do it correctly and quickly in the street. Think about it, Jack the Ripper had very minimal time, but knew exactly how to do everything he did. That's because he had practice, lots of practice. Our guy however, doesn't have the experience. Copycats generally only body dump. They very rarely commit the actual murder in the original location. It's almost impossible to do in the first place."

"Have you delved further into your crematory theory?"

"Not a whole lot, no."

"I'd like to take a look and see what I can find. We're like sitting ducks here anyway waiting for Inspector Thompson to return."

"Be my guest. I'd love to see what you find. I know there was at least one crematory within the London area during 1888. I believe it was called Woking Crematorium."

"Then I shall start there," Abner said.

~

Spencer was just about to order in lunch for herself and Abner when he called her over to his desk.

"It seems as though you are correct. The Woking Crematorium had its first official cremation in 1885. During that year they only saw three cremations. In 1886, they only had ten cremations and then in 1888 twenty-eight cremations took place. There is a good possibility that if Jack were working there during those five months in 1888 he could have had access to the bodies. In my general knowledge of the process, when cremation is chosen, the family chooses a coffin and then the body is never seen again, only the coffin until cremation. They almost never open that coffin again. It's traditionally very different from burial ceremonies and such where the body is on display so to speak. He would have had access to the bodies and been able to mutilate them without anyone knowing and since they were cremated there is really no way of ever knowing."

"How far away is Woking from London?" Spencer asked.

"Oh nearly an hour I'd say with traffic or on the train. Maybe thirty miles."

"That was too far to travel for a daily commute, he would've had to move to the area."

"Yes. Are you thinking there may be victims in that area?" Abner asked.

"No. Abigail Bigsby lived in the Whitechapel or perhaps Hackney area. That I'm sure of. He only killed in that area because it reminded him of her. No, I was thinking on a different path entirely. What if perhaps he found out that Abigail aborted the child as he said in the letter, and what if that was in February. Remember she disappeared. He was so distraught he stabbed Annie Millwood a bunch of times and ran off, but that wasn't enough. So, he stabbed Ada Wilson in the throat nearly a month later. Still not satisfied and carrying around so much anger and pain he moved to Woking and thus took a job at the crematorium. That's where he learned about the anatomy and he did it all on his own. I wonder how many of those twenty-eight bodies that were cremated in 1888 were women and of those how many were during the months of April through July."

"I'm not sure. I'll see what I can find out," Abner said, typing on his laptop.

"When he felt comfortable enough, he left Woking and returned to Whitechapel to carry out the destruction he planned on Abigail, but couldn't find her, so he found others to take her place."

"That is feasible. It definitely makes sense. Remember he was not a doctor and a butcher wouldn't know about humans, only animals so that theory is out the door."

"Exactly my point," Spencer replied.

"Listen to this, in the United Kingdom a body is never removed from the coffin once it arrives at the crematorium from the undertaker. It's against the law. The body must be cremated within seventy-two hours after the funeral service."

"That would have been the perfect set up for him especially in 1888. There probably weren't many people willing to take on that kind of job and his duties were probably shoveling coal into the furnace and moving coffins inside and so forth. I'm sure he was there alone and that would've provided ample time for him to learn all about the human anatomy without ever being noticed. As I have said before, he was a smart man."

"How do you think our ghost learned his skills? Surely, crematoriums are monitored more closely these days," Abner said.

"Oh, I'm sure they are. I believe our guy may actually have a bit of medical knowledge. Maybe he started medical school and worked on cadavers possibly but either quit or was kicked out at one time. He could also be a medical assistant, working specifically with autopsies. That could also give him the knowledge and practice. He's had time to study JTR. This isn't something he decided to do overnight," Spencer stated.

"I believe he may have even quit his job to pursue this infatuation. Maybe we could check with local mortuaries and hospitals to see if anyone fitting our description was employed there within the past year."

"That's actually a good idea, Abner. We can run it by Inspector Thompson when he returns. I'd like to see if I can get a little more information out of those two women first. It's possible we may get an even better description of him."

"Do you think Inspector Thompson will take the time to check those places for our suspected ghost's employment?"

"If he doesn't, I will," Spencer said. "If he gets these prostitutes to speak with me, then surely he will do a little extra investigating. He is by all means the actual detective here."

"Have you ever thought of becoming a detective yourself?" Abner asked.

Spencer laughed. "No. Not in the least bit. I don't play well with the politics that go on in a police department. I'd much rather be on the outside. Do you see me obeying orders from someone that couldn't find a clue if I gave it to them? I don't think so. The FBI was much different than a regular police department. What about you?"

"Me? Oh heavens no. I'm a history professor. I tend to lean more towards Criminal History which has led to my authoring numerous non-fiction books, but I've never wanted to be a part of Scotland Yard. That would literally be the last job on Earth that you would find me in. I promise you that."

Chapter Fourteen

Inspector Thompson knocked loudly and rang the bell over and over at 27 White Church Lane. "Oh, calm down," he said to the woman next to him.

"I don't like being seen with you. It's bad for business. Besides, I told you I don't know anything else," the eager woman replied. She watched the street from both ends hoping no one recognized her.

Abner shuffled down the stairs in his night clothes. He fumbled for the door locks in the near darkness.

"Who is pounding on the door at this hour?" Spencer growled from the bottom of the stairs. She was dressed in unflattering flannel pajamas and her hair was sticking out in all directions.

"I believe it is Inspector Thompson," Abner replied as he pulled the door open.

"Dr. Montague, pardon my intrusion, but it seems to have taken me most of the day to find this woman and there was no way I could confine her until morning. Is Ms. Donovan available?" Inspector Thompson walked inside with the scantily dressed woman. Abner nearly gasped at the amount of skin showing under the overcoat she was wearing.

"I'm right here," Spencer yawned, stepping into the room.

"Please forgive me for arriving at this late hour," Inspector Thompson said.

"I understand. Give me a minute to change clothes."

"I too shall change into something a bit more decent, please excuse me." Abner followed her up the stairs.

Spencer returned a few minutes later wearing a light blue sweater, dark blue pants, and black slip on shoes. She'd brushed her teeth and combed her hair hastily after redressing. Abner appeared just behind her wearing a dark brown pants suit. Spencer figured he must have dressed in record time.

"This is Sheryl Smith. Ms. Smith, this is Dr. Abner Montague and Ms. Spencer Donovan. As I told you, they have some questions about the night you were attacked," Inspector Thompson said.

"Please, have a seat, Ms. Smith. May I get you anything?" Abner held his hand out to the chair in front of his desk.

She plopped down in the seat, shaking her head no.

"Ms. Smith, did you see the man that attacked you?" Spencer asked.

"Briefly. I opened the door, asked him a question, and the next thing I know he snatched me, spun me around, and stabbed me right here in the throat," she said pointing to the scar on her neck. "It happened so fast I couldn't scream."

"Do you remember what he looked like? Clothes? Facial hair? Any of the such?"

"He was wearing dark clothes and a hat like an old gangster hat."

"Good. Anything else?"

"I don't know. There was only a small light on in the room. Everything about him was dark though. I do remember that. He may have had facial hair, but he could've just been dirty too. It happened so fast."

"I understand. I want you to think back to when he grabbed you. How tall would you say he was?"

"I don't know my back was to him." She shrugged.

"Where do you think your head came to on his body?"

"I have no idea."

"How tall are you, Ms. Smith?"

"Five foot two, but five foot five with my heels on."

"What were you wearing the night of your attack?"

"I was...I was barefoot," she stated.

"Inspector Thompson, how tall are you?"

"Six foot with my shoes on."

"Good, I want to do a little experiment if you will. Ms. Smith please stand with your back to Inspector Thompson just as you did the night of your attack." Spencer waited for them to get into position. "Wonderful, now do remember if his chin was near the top of your head or much higher like the inspectors?"

"He was definitely not as tall as the inspector. In fact, I remember his breath on my head so his mouth must have been close."

"Inspector Thomas, would you please breathe hard as if she were struggling to get away?" Spencer waited a minute. "Do you feel his breathe on you, Ms. Smith?"

"No, not at all."

"Good, you can let her go, Inspector. Dr. Montague, please take the position behind Ms. Smith and mimic the same heavy breathing."

"I definitely feel him breathing on my head. The guy that attacked me was much closer to this height. I think maybe a little taller though. I don't remember his face being this close."

"Excellent. Thank you, Dr. Montague. One more question for you, Ms. Smith. Did he speak to you?"

"Yes, he said 'this won't take long'. I remember his voice being deep and sort of scratchy sounding like he'd been out in the cold air all night. It was also very low. I barely heard him."

"Thank you for seeing us, Ms. Smith," Spencer said.

"No problem. I hope you catch the rat bastard," she exclaimed.

"I need to take her back. I'll return with the other woman shortly. She's expecting me," Inspector Thompson stated.

"Looks like we're in for a long night," Spencer muttered as Abner shut and locked the door.

"It appears that way. I do believe your height theory is correct."

"Yes. Based on what she was saying, I believe he is probably around five eight or five nine as I first predicted."

"That wouldn't put him much taller than the girls if they are in high heels, though."

"True, but all of the women except for this one more than likely got into his car. At that point it wouldn't matter if she were wearing shoes or not because her petite height would make it easy for him to subdue her in the car. I believe this other woman may give us a better idea of what he is doing since she rode in his car."

"I'm going to make some tea since the inspector should be returning shortly," Abner said. He knew better than to ask her after the hundredth time or so when she'd she finally told him she didn't want tea now or ever and to stop asking.

"I'm going to work on my notes. I'll let him in when he arrives," Spencer replied.

~

Close to two hours later, Inspector Thompson knocked on the door and rang the bell. Spencer rushed over, answering right away.

"I'm sorry it took me longer than expected," he said, nearly sneering at the woman next to him. Spencer glanced down at her. She was wearing some sort of skin tight dress that barely covered her extremities under a dingy old overcoat.

"Please come in." Spencer pulled the door wide. Abner was sitting in the chair behind his desk. He stood quickly, offering the seat to the woman.

"Cindy Smith, this is Dr. Abner Montague and Ms. Spencer Donovan. As I informed, they have some questions for you about your attack."

"Thank you for seeing us, Ms. Smith."

"Please call me Cindy and it seems as if I had no choice," she grimaced.

Spencer cleared her throat and peered down at her notes.

"Can you describe your attack for me?"

"I was walking along the sidewalk and a dark car stopped next to me. The window cracked a few inches and the lock clicked. I checked the streets and no one was around, so I got into the car."

"What did the car look like?" Spencer asked.

"It was dark with dark windows and a little older. The seats were cloth. I remember there were no interior lights. The gauges and everything were all dark."

"Okay. How many doors did it have?"

"Two."

"Was it an automatic or manual?"

"Automatic."

"Alright, so you got into the car. What happened next?"

"My memory is a little hazy. We didn't drive very far, only a few blocks. I remember asking him what he wanted me to do and he said 'tell everyone I'm back'. I barely heard him, his voice was deep and low, almost hollow sounding."

"What happened after he said that?"

"I don't know. He grabbed me and there was something wet on my face like he was holding something on me. I woke up in the alley with horrible pain and bleeding from the stab wounds in my stomach and legs."

"Do you remember any smells?"

"No. Everything went black within a second or two. It was so fast."

"Did you see what he looked like?"

"No. It was so dark in the car and he was dressed in dark clothes. I could barely make out a person sitting in the driver's seat. I think he may have been wearing a hat."

"Did you feel any facial hair when he grabbed you?"

Cindy shook her head no. "I think my head was under his chin not against his face."

"One more question about the car. Did you notice anything different about it? Special wheels or light covers?"

"No. It was a regular small dark car."

"Could you find it in a book of car pictures?" Inspector Thompson asked.

"I doubt it. I wasn't really looking at the car. I just noticed it stopped and I got in quickly."

"Thank you for speaking with us, Cindy," Spencer said.

"I shall return at some point today," Inspector Thompson informed.

"I have some new information for you to check out when you come back," Spencer replied.

"Then my return will be sooner than later I presume." Inspector Thompson walked out the door.

"It's fairly obvious he rendered her unconscious. This is how he is getting the women to his killing location," Abner voiced as he locked the door.

"Yes, it's also how he is able to handle them without any sound. I think he's probably using chloroform. It's a form of anesthesia that works quickly when inhaled. You don't need medical knowledge to pour it on a rag or towel and hold it over someone's nose and mouth. He could have acquired it working in the medical field if in fact he was working in a hospital or even a morgue. He possibly learned to make it at home."

"It's not as difficult to make as people think. There have been many killers that have used homemade versions," Abner added.

"I wish we had more to go on with the car. At first, I thought he was possibly dumping and stealing cars, but after our witnesses in the murder areas have described a similar car, he's probably using the same one over and over. He has to wonder by now if someone has seen him or his car. I mean he showed himself to two women that he left alive. Albeit it was dark and they wouldn't know him if he was standing next to them in the grocery store more than likely."

"They probably wouldn't know the car either. Remember when Inspector Thompson asked her if she could pick out the car? She pretty much said no."

"If I was stabbed a bunch of times in my stomach or in my throat I don't think I'd want to remember either. I wonder if these women know of each other? If so, it won't be long before they start connecting their attacks to these murdered women that keep popping up all over town."

"Inspector Thompson is trying desperately to keep all of these stories from becoming linked. He's right. The city would be in a major panic."

"I agree not to tell the entire city, but the women on the streets and in the brothels should know. Don't forget Sheryl Smith was attacked in her room and so was Mary Kelly. The threat is to all prostitutes not just the ones walking the streets."

"That is a fact. We should probably let the inspector know more about Mary Kelly. Maybe that will entice him to head warning to all of the women of the night."

~

The inspector returned rather hastily. The man looked as if he hadn't eaten nor slept in days and his pants suit looked like he had been in it for multiple days as well. He was wrinkled and ruffled inside and out.

"Pardon my appearance. It's been a rather trying night for me. I believe you have some new information," he said.

"That is correct. First of all, you're looking for a small statured man. He's not built very large, but is most definitely strong. He's also only about five foot eight or nine. He drives a dark car probably with very dark tinted windows."

"That's not a lot to go on," Inspector Thompson sighed.

"There's more," Abner stated.

"The local mortuaries and hospital morgues need to be checked for an employee fitting this description that may have quit earlier this year," Spencer said.

"That's absurd," the inspector huffed. "What has led you to believe he held a job here?"

"He had to learn his trade somewhere," Abner exclaimed.

"It's more than that. He lives here just like Jack the Ripper lived in his hunting ground. Serial killers don't stray far from home, Inspector. That's a fact that a person in your position should know."

Inspector Thompson sneered at her. "This could be a wild goose chase with no results."

"Yes, it very well could be, but it could also lead you to a suspect with a possible name and address," Spencer said. "If it's too much of a burden, Dr. Montague and I will gladly handle this affair."

"Of course," Abner agreed.

"No. That's not necessary. I need a few hours of sleep and I'll start checking them myself."

"Are you sure you don't want us to assist you?"

"No. It may only arouse suspicion."

"Speaking of suspicion," Spencer added. "We really think you should reconsider warning the prostitutes on the streets and in the brothels."

"There is no reason to stir up the streets with fear."

"You're quite wrong, Inspector. Let me show you something." Spencer opened a file on her desk and placed two black and white photos in front of him. She watched his eyes scan the pictures before he visibly grimaced.

"What is this?" he asked.

"That was Mary Kelly. She was Jack the Rippers supposed last victim. He went into her hostel room and completely mutilated her body. Multiple organs were found around the bed where he cut her face beyond recognition and literally skinned her like an animal. There was no noise made, no warning given. If you remember, Sheryl Smith was attacked in her room with no noise and no warning. Inspector Thompson, this is a very big reason why these women need to be cautioned to stay away from dark two-door cars and short statured men with dark features and fedora hats."

"I'll run it by my Chief Inspector and my superintendant, but I can't promise anything. They are pushing to close this case as soon as possible and with very little media involvement. That generally means no word on the street," Inspector Thompson exclaimed.

Chapter Fifteen

"Tomorrow is the twenty-seventh," Abner said, sipping his morning tea. He and Spencer had not heard from the inspector in two days. They were sitting in the office like bumps on a log, playing the waiting game.

"Yes, I know it is," Spencer replied.

"Do you think he will send a letter?"

"I have a strong feeling he will. He's followed the timeline consistently so far. Why stray now?"

"We should warn the inspector. That first letter went to the Central News Agency. It's possible Central News will receive one again, if in fact he decided to write one. This will surely cause an uproar across the city."

Spencer shrugged. She knew he was right, but at the same time she felt as though the people should know what was going on around them. Maybe then he wouldn't be such a ghost if people were actually looking for him.

"It's possibly this will cause an uprising of another vigilante group. That's surely something the metro police do not want. I'll ring him," Abner said, reaching for the phone on his desk. The doorbell rang as he waited for the line to be picked up.

"No need. It looks like he has finally returned." Spencer answered the door and stepped aside so Inspector Thompson could come in.

"I was just ringing you. We have some news for you."

"I believe I have some news of my own," the inspector said.

"Well, go on then." Abner waved his hand towards the open seat in front of Spencer's desk.

"I checked the hospitals and mortuaries, but no one remembers a man matching your description."

"It's possible he lived outside of London at the time. In fact, it's probably true. He's a smart man and has covered his tracks well, Inspector," Spencer replied.

"If it's out of my jurisdiction, I cannot help you without further cause. I did get permission to warn the brothels of a man with dark features driving a dark car that may be looking to cause women harm." He raised his hand when Spencer tried to speak. "I know, it's vague and seemingly useless information, but that's all Scotland Yard is willing to give."

"Well, you better go back and tell them the entire city is about to find out what's really going on in twenty-four hours," Spencer growled.

"What do you mean? What is she saying?" he asked Abner.

"You really know nothing about Jack the Ripper do you?" Spencer sighed.

"I'm afraid not. I haven't exactly had time for light reading recently," the inspector retorted sarcastically.

"Does anyone currently working at Scotland Yard know anything about him? I'm beginning to think this is a huge waste of my time."

"Surely, you don't mean that?" Abner questioned.

"Actually, Abner, I do. There is a ghost of a man in this city somewhere that is recommitting the same exact crimes that were carried out a hundred and twenty-five years ago verbatim. If anyone sitting on their ass at the damn office knew anything about Jack the Ripper, they would easily link these two cases with their eyes closed and know that tomorrow a letter will be sent to Central News from the killer and in typical media fashion Central News will broadcast it to the public. So, Inspector Thomson, you are about to have that citywide uproar on your hands whether you want it or not." Spencer shoved a copy of the *Dear Boss* letter supposedly written by Jack the Ripper across the desk.

"This man's gone mad," Inspector Thompson screeched after reading the letter. "Surely you don't think our current killer will send such a letter to the media."

"Anything is possibly when you have a copycat or a ghost or whatever the hell this person is. They are working from a script telling them exactly how to do everything and when to do it."

"I doubt the Chief knows anything about this. I must go and warn him. What else do I need to know?"

"In three days, he will kill two more women. One in Whitechapel and the other in the City of London. Expect a postcard written by him sent to the media a day later. Shall I go on?" Spencer asked impatiently.

"Where does it end?" Inspector Thompson rubbed his face with his hands clearly showing signs of stress.

"During the month of October there will be a total of four letters and a postcard. One of the letters will be with a box containing a human kidney, allegedly that of one of his victims. November ninth, he will brutally mutilate a women in her room as I described to you days ago. This is where Jack the Ripper supposedly stopped. No one really knows for sure."

Inspector Thompson stood and paced the small floor. "We must find him before all of this. But how? I am at my wits end. I have no idea how to catch a ghost. Do you, Ms. Donovan?"

"No. The only thing that comes to mind is a stake-out situation. You would need to get the City Police involved to accomplish that and even then, you could easily miss him coming or going."

"I assure you, the City Police will not be involved by our doing. If he does murder someone in their district that will surely become their case, not mine."

"Your chief will need to cross that bridge when we get to it then," Abner said.

"Have you ever thought of the idea that maybe he isn't working alone?" Inspector Thompson asked.

"No. He's definitely doing this by himself. That I can promise you, Inspector," Spencer said.

"I need to go inform my Chief of this new information. He will not be pleased. I will return when I can. Until then, if something else comes up ring me at the station house." Inspector Thompson slipped his hat on and walked out the door.

"That went about as well as a cat taking a shower," Abner huffed.

Spencer laughed.

"I think someone at Scotland Yard is scared to admit what is going on here and reluctant to use the Jack the Ripper name," Spencer said.

"Oh, I agree. Just the thought that he may be back is eerie enough I suppose."

"We have less than twenty-four hours. What shall we do?" Spencer asked.

"How about a friendly game of cribbage?"

"Sure. Why not?" Spencer smiled.

~

At nine-thirty a.m. the next morning, Inspector Thompson was once again banging on the door and ringing the bell. Abner looked across the room at Spencer who was sitting at her desk reading her notes.

"I bet the letter has arrived," he muttered, going towards the door.

"It sounds like it."

"This arrived at Central News just this hour," Inspector Thompson said, handing Spencer a letter sealed in plastic. "It does not contain prints and the stamp and envelope closure were both self-adhesive."

Spencer looked at the red ink on the antique style parchment paper. She placed it next to the original *Dear Boss* letter and was surprised by the similarities.

"He's either studied the old letters or his handwriting generally sucks," she said as she began reading the letter.

Dear Boss,

As you know, I have returned in rare form. I'm not hearing much from the police. I assume they don't want

118

anyone to know. Shame on them for keeping a secret such as this. I am once again ripping whores and shall not quit as I love my job. It's grand work I must say. Don't you think? I tried using my favorite ink but it dried too quickly. That would have been a jolly good time for the police. Do they still think I'm a doctor? Ha Ha I must get back to work, the glistening blade of my knife is calling to me.

Farewell Old Chap,

Ripper's Ghost

Spencer read the letter twice over before handing it to Abner.

"He doesn't say much, just like the first letter didn't really say much either. All of the letters have been theorized as hoaxes over the years," Spencer said. "The thing that does draw my attention, he's referring to himself as Ripper's Ghost. This coincides with my theory that he believes he is a reincarnation of Jack the Ripper or something of the sort."

"I agree. He's definitely not in the right state of mind," Abner added.

"Well, whatever or whoever he is, at least the central news agreed not to publish this if we gave them a story to run. The Chief is working on that now."

"That's good to hear. Did you get any word on setting up a stake-out?" Abner asked, handing the letter back to him.

"No. We don't have enough manpower for that. It can't be done."

"You could do it yourself or with a constable or another inspector. The night of the thirtieth a woman will be dumped sometime in the very early morning on Henrique Street, possibly near the school house. The second woman will be found in Mitre Square," Spencer stated.

"We can accompany you if you'd like, Inspector," Abner said.

"No, that won't be necessary. I will see what I can do."

30 SEPTEMBER 2013

The black car cruised slowly by Marjorie 'Margie' Rhodes as she sashayed back and forth on the corner. She waited at the corner after the car turned down the side street. The car rolled to a stop close to a hundred yards away, and Margie pulled her top down low enough to almost see her nipples as she walked towards the car. The windows were too dark to see inside, so she tried the door handle.

"Would you care for some company, sir?" she said when she pulled the door open. She couldn't see the driver very well, but noticed him nodding his head.

She sat down in the seat and barely had the door closed before he grabbed her, placing the rag over her face. She slumped down into the passenger seat as he drove away in silence. He glanced her way only once as the passing streetlights lit the interior of the car. He slowed down, turning on Henrique Street. The car came to a stop twenty yards from the school house. He left the car running with the lights off as he drug her limp body from the car to the sidewalk.

He positioned her flat on her back, drew a long, steel-bladed knife from the inside pocket of his overcoat, and knelt down beside her. Turning the blade over back and forth, he watched the edge shimmer in the moonlight before slicing it across her neck, severing the right artery. He backed away quickly, wiped the blade clean on the bottom of her clothes, and returned to his car, where he drove off into the night without looking back.

~

He checked the time on his pocket watch and was satisfied to see one a.m. was just passing. He turned down Commercial Street in time to see a woman walking alone. He slowed to a stop near the curb and waited.

Tabitha McPherson was just starting her night. She rarely walked the streets, but money was tight and the extra job or two she would pick up would be worth the risk of running into the Metro Police. She smiled and began walking swiftly when the dark car stopped close by.

She heard the locks click and slipped into passenger side quickly. There was no light in the car. She could only see a silhouette of the driver as he sped away, turning down the first side street. She glanced around and shrugged. She wasn't used to working in cars, but if that's what he wanted, she was fine with it. She began loosening her top.

"What pleasure are you seeking this evening?" she asked.

He wrapped his arms around her tightly, shoving the wet rag in her face as she started to scream while struggling to free herself. Within seconds the struggle ended. He fixed his position in the seat, adjusted his jacket and hat, and drove casually through the streets.

Arriving at his destination, he got out and unlocked the door, disappearing into the dark building, then returning for the unconscious woman a few minutes later. He carried her inside, placing her body in the center of the cold cement floor. The small lantern in the corner cast a soft glow over the woman and a shadow over the man kneeling in front of the steamer chest, searching the contents.

Finding what he was looking for, he held the perfect blade up to the dull light and sighed since he couldn't see the shine on the razor sharp edge. When the nearby woman began to stir, he moved over her, swiping the blade across her throat as her eyes began to open. He backed away, watching her body thrash for a second or two as the last of the blood spurted from the severed arteries. After she stopped moving, he knelt next to her upper body and wiped his blade clean. Then, he began cutting deep slanted gashes on her face, from her mouth to her eyes and back forming skin flaps. Finally, he cut through both of her eyelids and removed part of her nose.

He wiped his blade clean once again and moved lower next to her abdomen, pulling her dress up to her chest. He then made a long deep incision from her sternum down, curving beside her naval. The next cut divided the abdominal walls and took a horizontal course towards the right side and down the vagina to the rectum. The last long cut went in the opposite direction, opening the abdomen and exposing the bowels. He pushed the intestines to the side, revealing the liver before stabbing it on one side and cutting it vertically on the other side. He then cut her pancreas before slicing through the peritoneal lining and removing her left kidney. He placed the kidney in a glass jar filled halfway with red wine.

Afterwards, he cut the membrane lining of her uterus and removed part of her womb with the ligaments still attached, placing it on the floor next to him. He finished by cutting the top of both thighs through the frontal ligaments and back towards the rectum, then up again forming a flap on each side.

Satisfied with his work, he cleaned his blade and stowed it away in the chest. He disappeared outside to ready the car. Then, he carried her body out, placed her in the trunk, and drove towards Mitre Square inside the City of London.

He passed his drop location and circled back around a few minutes later when he saw a car parked down the street. The street was empty on his second pass so he pulled to the side and removed the body from the trunk, positioning her with her face to left and her arms by the side naturally. He pulled the intestines through the opening in the abdomen, cut off a short section, and placed that section along her side. He then put the remainder of the connected intestines over her shoulder before hurrying back to the car and driving off into the darkness.

Chapter Sixteen

Abner was sitting at his desk reading the newspaper and Spencer was reading the news online via her laptop.

"I wonder what's going on right now," Spencer pondered out loud.

"What do you mean?"

"Well, Inspector Thompson hasn't come barging through the door. I wonder what happened last night. Maybe he did stakeout the location and nab the guy and we just haven't heard yet."

"It's possible."

The loud knock on the door grabbed Spencer's attention. "Too good to be true, I'm guessing," she uttered under her breath, opening the door.

"He struck again. Two women as you suspected. The City Police have the second victim, but they are going to share information with us since we have the majority of the murders in our jurisdiction. They want everything though. I think the Chief's going to have a heart attack or stroke any moment now," he said, removing his hat and wiping his brow on his jacket sleeve.

"What did the scenes look like?" Spencer asked.

"Our victim only had her throat cut, but the one in the city was pretty cut up. I'll get everything to you as soon as I get my hands on it."

"Did you happen to make it out last night?" Abner asked.

"Yes. In fact, I was at the first location around midnight. I sat for a short while and saw nothing, so I moved to the second location. Sometime after three a.m. I saw a car pass by and turn down a side street. It was a dark car, but it was also fairly dark outside. I left soon after when I got the call that a body had been found. When I arrived, I noticed it was about a hundred and fifty yards from where I was sitting. The body was still warm with no signs of rigor mortis. She hadn't been there long, two hours at most," Inspector Thompson stated.

"What about the body in the city? Where was she found?"

"Mitre Square as you said she would be. A constable found her a couple hours later after I contacted the City Police to let them know there may be a murderer on the loose in the area."

"Were there any witnesses?" Abner asked.

"At this point, I do not know. I have no viable information. I shall return as soon as I have everything. It may not be until morning depending on when the autopsies are performed." Inspector Thompson put his hat back on his head and left once again.

"We need to figure out how to stop this madness, Abner."

"I agree, but how?"

"I have no idea. None at all." Spencer shrugged and rubbed her throbbing temples.

~

The next morning, Inspector Thompson arrived with a thick file folder in his hand. He walked inside, placing the folder on Spencer's desk before removing his hat.

"That's everything. Central News received word of the double murder and are now threatening to release the letter to the public," Inspector Thompson sighed. He looked tired and seemingly stressed.

Spencer opened the file and began comparing notes.

"That's definitely not the best thing to do. I hope your Chief has some authority over the media. I can't bear to imagine what will happen to the streets of London if they publish that letter," Abner said.

"I'm not sure how much leverage he has at this point."

"Both women fit the profile." Spencer turned to Abner. "They are prostitutes around forty years old and under five foot four. No DNA or prints were found on the bodies or at either scene. The woman in Mitre Square was Tabitha McPherson. She was known around the King's Cross area. She's definitely Catherine Eddowes all over again. Her face was mutilated, her bowels were thrown over her shoulder, part of her womb was missing, and her left kidney was missing as well. She was killed elsewhere and dumped very close to the original site. The woman killed on Henrique Street was Marjorie Rhodes. She frequented the Commercial Street and Victoria areas. She had her throat cut like Elizabeth Stride and she was killed right there on the sidewalk where she was found."

"That's different," Abner replied.

"Yes, maybe it was because he was only cutting her throat and didn't need the extra time. He felt comfortable there or he wouldn't have done it out in the open like that."

"That's a slap in our faces," Inspector Thompson said. "The fact that he felt at ease enough to cut a woman's throat on a sidewalk, near a school house of all places, is a huge defeat for the Metro Police. We should have men patrolling these streets all hours of the night."

"Why isn't that happening? I mean you basically know when and where he will strike every time, yet you're always two steps behind him."

"Budget cuts, I'm afraid. We are only operating with a small group of constables and they get tied up with domestic cases or accidents, you name it. That takes them away from patrolling for this madman," he huffed in frustration.

"Does your Chief just think he will stop like Jack did? That's absurd. He's not exactly following Jack's path. Who knows how long this will go on unless you catch him," Spencer said.

"If I had answers, I'd give them to you and if I knew of a way to catch him I'd run him up the flagpole by his neck," Inspector Thompson growled. "Forgive me, Ms. Donovan. The pressure of stopping this man is beginning to drive me over the edge."

"No need to apologize, Inspector. I personally think he needs his own neck cut through."

Inspector Thompson excused himself and stepped outside when his cell phone rang.

Spencer and Abner flipped through the file on the two newly murdered women. The autopsies both reported that the wounds were caused by a long sharp knife and both causes of death were severing of the carotid artery. The abdominal mutilation on the second woman was done post-mortem just as it had with all of the others.

"Do you think he's going to mail the kidney?" Abner asked.

"I don't know, but if I had to guess, I would say yes."

"The original kidney went to Lusk, but there is no longer a vigilante group. Who will he send it to?"

"Inspector Thompson or maybe Central News," Spencer replied.

"That will surely get their attention I presume."

"You know, at first I found it eerie that we were dealing with Jack the Ripper's ghost. Then, I was completely intrigued by the case. Now, I just want to catch this son of a bitch," Spencer said.

"I'm not sure what causes a person to want to hurt other people, and mimicking something as gruesome and horrendous as Jack the Ripper murders means we are dealing with a very sick individual. It's amazing how predictable his moves are, yet he hasn't been caught. It's going to take a drastic move by the Metro Police and I'm afraid they may not have any drastic moves in their repertoire."

"I'm starting to agree with you," Spencer replied as the door opened.

Inspector Thompson walked back inside with his head hung low. "It appears as if the Central News has received a postcard this morning signed Ripper's Ghost. I need to get over there straight away. I'll try to get a copy to you this evening," Inspector Thompson said, before leaving hastily.

"I was wondering when the postcard would appear," Abner muttered.

"I'm interested in seeing what it says. I wonder if he's going to hint at Whitehall."

"You think he's going to do it? Dump a torso?" Abner asked.

"Why not? He's following his own plan that coincides with the Whitechapel murders and Jack the Ripper murders."

"Do you think we should stakeout the Whitehall location tomorrow night?"

"I don't think it's a bad idea." Spencer looked up at him.

"What about Inspector Thompson?"

"I plan to let him know, but I'm sure with their budget cuts and everything else we will be alone."

~

Inspector Thompson appeared again just before Abner and Spencer headed up to the flat for the evening. He handed a photo copy of the postcard to Spencer.

"It was mailed from the same postal code and it has a few postal worker prints on it, but unless he's a postal worker, it's not worth much," he said.

Spencer looked at the paper on her desk. The ink was the same red color as the letter and the handwriting was almost identical.

Saucy Jack promised not to disappoint you, dear old boss. You'll soon hear of the double event. Oh the hounds in the Yard do make it so easy for me. I hope you enjoy my work as much as I enjoy it. I must get back to it. I have something very impressive in store for you next. I can't wait. Can you?

Ripper's Ghost

"I know the double event he's referring to is the two murders. I don't like the way he's taunting the police by saying we make it easy for him." Inspector Thompson sat down in the chair by Spencer's desk.

Spencer pushed the paper back across the desk towards him.

"He saw you the other night and dumped that body when you left. That's why he said the hounds are making it easy for him. He's a very smart man, as I've stated time and time again."

"Any idea what's going to be so impressive that he's speaking of?" the inspector asked.

"The Whitehall Torso," Spencer sighed.

"What in the hell is that?" he asked.

"On October second the torso of a woman was found at the New Scotland Yard building that was under construction. It is strongly believed that Jack the Ripper was not involved with that murder," Abner answered.

"Then why is he speaking of it?"

"He's not recreating only Jack the Ripper murders. I've explained the Whitechapel murders to you, Inspector. He has an array of murders from 1888 to 1891that he is capable of copying. You cannot narrow him down to only the JTR murders or you will never find him," Spencer said.

"So you're saying he's going to leave a torso at the Norman Shaw Buildings in the early hours of the morning?"

"Yes. Most likely the north building."

"The Chief is not going to buy this idea. The M.O. is totally wrong," Inspector Thompson said.

"That's not my problem." Spencer shrugged. "I have given you everything three steps ahead of the game, Inspector. If you truly intend to catch this ghost, then I suggest you take a good look at the Whitechapel murders too and make your own judgments. Abner and I will be near the north building later tonight."

"I'd advise against that for both of your safety." The inspector stood, putting his hat on as he turned towards Spencer. "If I cannot be in the area this evening, I will try my best to have a constable nearby."

Abner and Spencer watched him leave.

"He won't be there," she said.

"What makes you think that?"

"Call it intuition." She smiled.

"Do you think it's him?"

"Who? The killer? Inspector Thompson? No. He doesn't fit the profile. I think he's just following the Yard protocol and taking the heat of the investigation at the same time. This case is way over his head. You don't think it's him, do you?" she asked.

"I have to admit, I've thought about it."

"He's nearly six foot tall with reddish brown hair. You've seen his handwriting. It's not a match. Nothing about him fits the profile, Abner."

"I know. I guess I'm beside myself on how little Scotland Yard is doing to solve this case. It appears as if they're grasping at straws."

"If it is Inspector Thompson committing these murders, I will personally tear my criminology degree into pieces and become a cashier."

Abner laughed.

2 OCTOBER 2013

He walked down into the dimly lit room at the end of the long hallway and peered down at the nude woman laying on the metal table. Her throat was slit and her head was surrounded by dried blood that ran off the sides into a drain. It had been close to twenty-fours since he'd picked her up from the streets and watched her bleed to death.

He had been preparing for this victim for some time. Over a month ago, he placed a metal table with a drain similar to an autopsy table in the room, along with several sharp saws and knives that glimmered in the low light.

He went to work removing her arms first. Starting with the right one, he cut a jagged line around the upper arm where it connected with the shoulder socket. Next, he cut the muscle down to the bone and used the saw to slice through the bone. He tossed the arm on the floor and moved on to the left arm. Then, he detached both of her legs, putting them in the same pile with the arms.

He went back to the body and began sawing through the cut he had already made in her neck. Her head rolled to the side when it was freed. He grabbed the long hair, tossing the head into the pile on the floor and wiped his tools clean on a nearby towel.

He grinned in satisfaction at the bare torso lying in the middle of the table, before wrapping it like a Christmas or birthday present in thick brown paper. He used clear packing tape to close the ends and immediately took it out to the trunk of his car. When he walked back inside, he dug her arms out of the pile and wrapped them the same way and placed them in the trunk.

~

He took joy in riding around near Parliament and Westminster Abbey with the packages in the trunk. He finally headed over to his destination, parking by the curb near the front of the Norman Shaw Building. He got out and quickly placed the torso package on the top step, leaning it against the door of the building. He was pulling away from the curb when he noticed a little yellow car coming down the road. He drove through town for a few minutes winding back and forth until he was sure the little car was not following him.

He circled back towards the Thames and parked near the river boat landing. He removed the package of arms from the trunk and walked down close to the pier, placing the package on the bank. Then, he went back to his car and disappeared into the night.

Chapter Seventeen

Spencer and Abner parked down by Derby Gate, but kept riding by the Norman Shaw Buildings every thirty minutes.

"He could ride by here and dump her at any time," Abner said.

"Yes I know, but he will do it, eventually."

Abner turned down Victoria Embankment to once again ride past the buildings. It was close to three a.m. and they'd passed by at least a half a dozen times.

"What's that up ahead?" Spencer questioned, squinting to see through the darkness.

Abner pressed the gas a little harder.

"It's a car!" Spencer shouted. "Follow him!"

Abner floored the gas pedal in the electric car. They were a good two hundred yards behind him as he turned down Northumberland Avenue, where he went through the roundabout, and onto St. Martin's Place which turned into Charing Cross Road.

"We need to go faster," Spencer growled.

"It doesn't go any faster," Abner huffed.

When the dark car pulled off onto Great Newport Street, the battery gauge in Abner's car moved into the red area. They'd been driving for hours without charging the small car and the battery was almost depleted. Their car slowed to a stop as the dark car turned on Mercer Street and vanished.

"Son of a bitch!" Spencer yelled, smacking the dash with her fist.

"We should have charged it for a bit."

"Charged it my ass! We should've been in a real car!" She got out and walked a few feet away to blow off steam. When she returned to the car, Abner was on the phone with Inspector Thompson. "Tell him to go down to the Thames, probably near one of the piers. The arms should be there somewhere."

Abner gave him the information and hung up the phone. "He's heading there now. He sent a constable to assist us."

"Yeah," she said sarcastically.

"I know you're upset. I am too. We were so close. It's unfortunate the battery died, but you can't blame the car. Electric cars are becoming more popular every year."

"Tomorrow, I'm getting a rental car that runs on gas," Spencer growled.

~

The constable finally showed up a half hour later with a temporary charger that boosted the battery long enough for them to drive to a charging station close by. An hour later, the battery was charged enough to drive across town, so they drove back to the office to make notes on the dark car they saw and the direction it traveled in.

Inspector Thompson was at the door just after sunrise. Abner and Spencer were both asleep. The repeated pounding on the door and ring of the bell finally woke them.

"I'm sorry to wake you both," he apologized, noticing their attire. Abner was in a button down two piece pajama top and bottoms and Spencer was in a tee shirt and pajama pants.

"What did you find?" Spencer asked.

"There was a female torso wrapped in heavy paper and tape on the doorstep of the Norman Shaw Building to the north and a pair of arms seemingly wrapped the same way, was found on the river bank by the Westminster Pier. The preliminary autopsy shows the arms belong to the torso. I'll have more later today."

"We were so damn close," Spencer huffed.

"What happened?" the inspector asked.

"We saw the dark car driving away from the curb near the north building and we followed for a few miles and Abner's electric car petered out on us," she said sarcastically.

"You drive an electric car?" he asked Abner.

"Yes, I do. There is nothing wrong electric cars. I do believe I read recently that within the next two years part of the Metro Police fleet will be using electric cars."

Inspector Thompson shrugged. "I have no idea, but I can assure I will be driving a gas powered car."

"I ordered a rental that should be delivered today," Spencer said.

"Are you sure that was our guy?"

"I'd bet my life on it," Spencer replied.

"Did he know you were following him?"

"I don't know. It's hard to tell. He was a pretty good distance away since again the electric banana only goes so fast."

The inspector laughed and Abner rolled his eyes with his chin in the air.

"Well, it may be a good idea to change vehicles for a bit, just in case he did notice you. We don't need either of you becoming a target." Inspector Thompson wrote on a small notepad he pulled from his pocket. "Where did you lose him?"

"Mercer Street, but he could live anywhere. I still have a feeling he's working and possibly living in Spitalfields."

"What makes you think that?"

"The woman he killed and dumped near Hanbury Street. She has a very distinct timeline that has to include a short car ride. That means he killed her close by and we know he didn't kill her out in the open so he's obviously working out of a building of some sort."

"There's an abundance of abandoned buildings all over the various areas of London."

"Yes, I know. It's very easy to hide out in this city."

"I need to get back to the station. I'll let you know as soon as I know something. Maybe he left us some evidence this time," Inspector Thompson said.

"I'm going back to sleep. Wake me when my car arrives," Spencer told Abner.

~

Later that afternoon, Inspector Thompson arrived with the autopsy report for the torso and arms. Spencer grabbed the folder and began reading the report. She stopped midway through and shuffled the papers on her desk until she found the report on the Whitehall Mystery, and placed it side by side with the new report.

"The body was just beginning to decompose on the edges. She'd been dead over twenty-four hours. The wounds are fresh, so the removal of the head and limbs was fairly recent, probably right before she was dumped." Spencer paused to scan the rest of the page.

"She was in her thirties with pale skin and dark hair, and stood around five foot three inches with a slender build. The arms found on the river bank appeared to match the torso when held together and DNA confirmed the match. There is no cause of death listed, and as of now her identity is unknown."

"My chief is having a hard time believing this is the same guy. Everything about this crime scene and body are completely different from the others," Inspector Thompson said. "But, I've been on those websites you mentioned and I have to agree with you that he's recreating a lot more than the initial Jack the Ripper murders."

"What do you plan to do about it?" Abner asked.

"I went against direct orders and I have put together a small search group of myself and a handful of constables. We're going to begin searching abandoned flats this afternoon."

"What area are you starting in?" Spencer asked.

"Stepney," he replied.

"What about Spitalfields?"

"I know you think he's in Spitalfields, but what makes you so sure?" Inspector Thompson questioned.

"I truly believe Jack lived in Spitalfields and it's possible this guy feels the same way. You have to remember we are dealing with a very smart man that obviously believes he is Jack the Ripper. He will want to live and breathe and lie in the same place as his mentor. You can start in Stepney, but I really think that is the wrong direction."

"I'll take a look at the map this evening and adjust my plan accordingly if I see fit to do so," he said.

"There is one thing you should know," Abner added.

"What is that?"

"You may receive Tabitha McPherson's left kidney in the mail."

"What?"

"Someone mailed a piece of Catherine Eddowes kidney to George Lusk who was head of the Vigilante Committee in October of 1888. We have a feeling you may be the addressee this time if our guy stays true to his mailings. We already know he took the woman's kidney."

"Isn't that just jolly wonderful," the inspector huffed.

"Have you used the same coroner for all of the victims in Whitechapel?"

"Yes. He also observed the autopsy of Tabitha McPherson in the city morgue. Why do you ask?"

"If his name is known in connection with this case he may be the recipient of the mailing instead of you."

"I will handle that situation when I get to it. Until then, I have flats to check," Inspector Thompson said. He put his hat on and left the office.

"Do you think he's moving in the right direction?" Abner asked, lighting his pipe.

"No. I think he's going to waste his time by starting in Stepney. Not to mention, I doubt our guy is using an abandoned house."

"I don't think he's in a flat either," Abner agreed. "He comes and goes in the middle of the night with bodies. If he had neighbors, someone would have noticed him by now. I think he's in some kind of old building. I know you feel strongly about Spitalfields and your theory about Beverly Coleman's timeline could be true, so you may be correct. That would've been the ideal area for Jack to live in for sure and based on your family history, the women all came from that area."

"Where do you think he is?" Spencer asked.

"If I had to guess, he's where there is no risk of being seen. That makes me think he's on the outskirts away from the city and Whitechapel, maybe somewhere like Hackney."

"You think he's that far out?"

Abner shrugged.

"He's grabbing women from Victoria and occasionally Commercial Street. I know those areas are close to Spitalfields, but Hackney is between Victoria and Spitalfields so it's closer to his hunting ground. The only woman he picked up in King's Cross was the woman dumped in Mitre Square. He probably did that because he had already picked up someone from close to home and cut her throat on the very same sidewalk. The area was hot and he needed new grounds. I think he picked up Tabitha McPherson in King's Cross, took her to the place he works, mutilated her, drove right through the hot zone with her in the trunk of his car, and dumped her in Mitre Square."

"That's a pretty good theory, Abner."

"You've said it yourself, he's smart and he's obviously toying with Scotland Yard just like JTR did."

"If you're right, the inspector is miles away from the search area if he starts in Stepney. He needs to be concentrating between Spitalfields and Hackney."

"Give him a few days to prove himself wrong. He'll be back with no results and want to know more about the areas we have in mind and the types of buildings. He seemingly came up with this idea on his own and is beating his proud chest at the moment," Abner said.

Chapter Eighteen

A week went by before Abner and Spencer heard from Inspector Thompson. He was only successful in finding homeless people in his search of abandoned flats in Stepney. None of them fit the profile and there were no traces of evidence or dark cars in the area. He finally agreed to move his search to the area between Hackney and Spitalfields and start searching buildings instead of flats.

"You better both be correct. I've just about exhausted all of my resources," Inspector Thompson said.

"They wouldn't be exhausted if you had listened to us in the first damn place," Spencer growled.

"I do believe that I am a Detective Inspector, Ms. Donovan. I do know how to do my job, very well actually."

"Could've fooled me."

"I think we're all a bit exhausted with this entire case," Abner said.

Inspector Thompson snatched his hat from the desk. "I'll let you know if I find anything."

Spencer watched him leave, wishing she could slap him in the back of the head. "Why are police detectives so damn ignorant?" she huffed.

"I have no idea." Abner shrugged.

"Let's take a drive while it's still daylight out. I want to ride around the area and take a look at the buildings. Maybe something will stand out."

"I'll go fetch the car," Abner said, snubbing out his pipe. He grabbed his coat and hat from the rack next to the door.

"Do not return with that electric thing you call a car."

"I know. I know," he sighed, shaking his head.

~

Spencer and Abner drove around for hours looking at most of the main streets and side streets from Spitalfields to Hackney. None of the buildings looked any different than the next and there were a number of dark cars on the road that blended into the traffic. It wasn't as simple as she hoped it would be. She stared out the window at the concrete landscape as Abner drove. The panic light was starting to come on. She wondered how much longer it would be before they got ahead of this ghost. How many more women would have to die? She wondered what her life was going to be like when she finally went home after working the case of her lifetime. Nothing would ever be the same.

"I say we head back. It'll be dark soon anyway," Abner said.

"Stop at that store on the corner by the office. I need more coffee for the morning," Spencer replied.

"Shall I stop at the bakery for pastries as well?"

"If you want to. Abner, you don't need my approval to have a pastry," she laughed. "We're not married, at least I don't think I've been here long enough for common law. Have I?"

Abner cleared his throat nervously, straightening his jacket as he stared straight ahead.

"Oh Abner, it was a joke. Calm down. You're not my type anyway and you're old enough to be my father or perhaps my grandfather."

"I beg your pardon. I'm not quite that old," he huffed.

"Then you can enjoy a pastry and if it bothers you that much, we can go to mass and repent our pastry obsession this weekend."

"Are all Americans as sarcastic and rude as you?"

"I'd like to think most of them are worse than me. I take it you've never been to New York City."

"I've never been to America at all," he said. "It's too busy and snobbish for me."

Spencer laughed. "I do believe England has their fair share of snobs. I've had a few English noses turned up at my American accent since I've been here."

"I have never done such a thing," Abner gasped.

Spencer grinned and rolled her eyes. "Do you need anything?" she asked as the car stopped near the store.

"No, thank you. I will do my shopping this weekend."

"Suit yourself. I'll be back in a few minutes." Spencer got out of the car and darted across the street towards the small store. She was surprised to see the car missing when she walked outside with her bag. She was about freak out when she saw the white rental car coming down the street from the opposite direction.

"Did you go for a spin around the block?" she questioned, sliding into the passenger seat.

"I took it upon myself to run down to the tea shop and I also stopped for pastries," Abner replied.

"So the tea bags they sell in this store are different from the ones down the street?"

"Oh, they're dreadful. You cannot get good tea from a grocer. Everyone knows that."

"Apparently, I didn't." Spencer rolled her eyes and smiled. The old, English cod was growing on her.

~

Three days later, Inspector Thompson was banging on the door in the middle of the afternoon. Abner rushed around his desk to answer the absurd knocking and was just about rundown by the inspector as the door opened.

"This arrived for me with the mail carrier yesterday morning," he said, placing a folder on Spencer's desk.

She opened the folder, revealing a couple of pictures and a copied letter. Examining the pictures further, she noticed it was a bloody red blob wrapped in paper and mailed in a box.

"I'm assuming this is part of a woman's kidney?"

"You are correct. The coroner has it at the moment. I believe it's a match for Tabitha McPherson."

Spencer nodded and read the letter.

From Hell

Mr. Thompson,

Ripper's Ghost

I send you half of the kidney I took from a woman. This should really get you hounds moving I suppose. I would send you my knife, but I need it again soon. I hope you're enjoying my work, as I am having a jolly good time doing it.

Catch me if you can,

Ripper's Ghost

"It's about what I expected," Spencer said.

"There's something else," he added.

Spencer looked up at him.

"They've found a hair either on the organ or inside the box I'm not sure which."

"When will you know more?" Spencer asked.

"Well the body is the property of the City Police and the killer sent this to me at the Yard, so we have a bit of a clustered situation at the moment," he replied.

"When will you have the DNA report on the hair?" Abner asked.

"It's top priority, so probably tomorrow morning."

"I'd like to take a look at it when you get it."

"Sure."

"It's possible that this hair is our killers, but it could very well be from the person that opened the box. Did you open the box, Inspector Thompson?"

"Yes, I did. So, if it's my hair then we have nothing."

"Precisely," Abner said.

"How are the searches going?" Spencer asked.

"About as useless and time consuming as the first search in Stepney. There are just too many places to search and not enough man hours, I'm afraid it may be a lost cause."

"Don't quit now. You've come too far. He knows you're the one looking for him. The game has officially begun," Spencer said.

"What game?"

"Inspector Thompson, are you a chess playing man?"

"No. It's not a game I've ever given much thought to. Why?"

"This game is known as murder chess. He is on one side of the board and you are on the other. Until now, he was playing the board alone. You've given him an opponent."

"Is that a good thing or a bad one?"

"It could work in your favor or his."

"Wonderful. I've had enough riddles for the day. I'll return to you when I have the DNA report." Inspector Thompson bid farewell and left the office.

"We need to look closely at that report if it's his hair," Abner said.

"I still don't think it's him. That's too easy," Spencer replied.

"This will be confirmation either way, do you not agree?"

"No, I agree. If his hair was inside the wrapping then we may have reason to believe he's involved. If it was just inside the box or on the box the we have to go with reasonable doubt."

"Ah, ever the prosecutor," Abner said, raising his pipe and nodding his head in her direction. "We shall see soon enough I presume."

"If it is the inspector, I will be truly shocked. He will have done an award winning job playing the idiot detective card and quite possibly be the smartest serial killer I have ever come in contact with."

"You mentioned the murder chess game. What a match it has been if he is our killer," Abner exclaimed.

"Chess game of a lifetime, for sure," Spencer agreed.

Abner puffed his pipe. "Do you think he will tamper with evidence? Maybe give us a false report?"

"Unfortunately, there is no way of knowing for sure. If it's him, he will slip up. You can only play both sides of the board for so long."

"This could be why he started his search in the opposite direction. He was trying to throw us off his trail," Abner said.

"Yes, but he's now searching the correct area."

"Or so he says he is. Even if he is searching Spitalfields and Hackney, he could easily go in and out of the building he's working in and call it a 'cleared' building."

"I really don't think he fits the profile. He's too tall, he's pale with red hair and a matching red mustache. All of the witnesses say the man had dark features. Plus, I think you're missing a huge clue. He brought both of the attack victims to us personally. One of the women definitely saw her attacker and neither woman looked at him any different."

"Have you seen your Hollywood movies? There are very spot-on disguises available. It could be a dark wig and glued on dark facial hair or perhaps something like paint to make his face look darker."

"Abner, you do know if Inspector Thompson is Jack the Ripper's ghost, we are in a world of shit and my career is flushed down the toilet."

"How so?"

"Because he's been working next to us on this case from the very beginning and we could've prevented so many murders."

"We weren't looking at him that way in the beginning," Abner said.

"This conversation is giving me a hell of a headache. I need to clear the cobwebs from my head. Let's go down to that pub around the block."

"I haven't been there in a number of years. I guess a good scotch would be nice."

~

The next morning Spencer was eating aspirin like candy and nursing a hangover. She should have thought twice about matching the old man drink for drink. She didn't hear any noise in the flat and wondered how he was fairing. She was surprised to see his bed was already made up for the day. She took a hot shower and slowly made her way downstairs.

"I was beginning to worry," Abner said.

"How long have you been up? And why don't you have a headache from hell too?"

"The English hold their liquor much better." He grinned.

"Uh huh, sure you do. I'm English born and Irish before American, so that's just a bunch of bullshit."

"Do all women in American use such foul language?"

"Are all Englishmen pain in the ass old cod's like you?"

He laughed.

"Any word from the inspector?"

"No-" The knocking on the door cut Abner off. "That sounds like him."

"Here's your report," Inspector Thompson said, handing the file to Abner at the door. He walked inside and removed his hat.

Abner read the report.

"Your hair was in the box," he said to the inspector.

"Yes."

"How did your hair get into the box?" Spencer asked.

"I guess when I opened it."

"There was a second hair found inside the paper wrapping," Abner said. "The DNA isn't in the system."

"Is the hair human?"

"What do you mean?" the inspector asked.

"Was it synthetic like wig hair or possibly horse hair? I know they makes wigs from horse hair too."

"The DNA report is for a human. A white male to be exact," Abner said. "Do you know what database they used for the search?" he asked the inspector.

"London Proper."

"Do you mind if I keep this report?"

"No. I don't see why not. I need to get going. The Chief has called a meeting at the Yard this morning," the inspector replied on his way out.

"It's not him," Abner said.

"If he's using a wig made of human male hair it could very well be him," Spencer countered.

"Now, you believe my theory?" Abner asked.

"No, I didn't say that. I said 'if' and 'could'. I still don't think he is our killer. What are you going to do with that report?"

"I'm going to see if my friend at the University can run it in larger databases. He works at the lab in the medical department. I don't know if he can, but it's worth a try."

"There's a possibility it may not show up at all if he's never been arrested in connection to other crimes."

"That's true, but we were lucky enough to get some kind of evidence this time and I believe we should try everything under the sun to identify him," Abner stated.

Chapter Nineteen

Two days later, Spencer was working on her murder profile. Trying to fit Inspector Thompson into the boxes was proving easier than she originally thought. Abner was called away earlier that morning, so she was patiently awaiting his return. She was a little excited and a little terrified that she may have been in such close contact with the Ripper's Ghost this entire time.

Abner walked through the office door with a somber look on his face. Spencer stood up and walked over to him.

"Is everything okay? I've been working on the profile all morning and I think I've fit Inspector Thompson into our suspects role."

He placed a manila envelope on his desk and removed his hat and overcoat, hanging them on the rack.

"You need to sit down, Abner. You look pale," Spencer said.

"No, I'm afraid you need to sit down," he replied to her.

"Why? What's happened?"

Abner waited for her to sit before opening the envelope. He removed the few pieces of paper. "Inspector Thompson's not our ghost," he paused and sighed. "Your brother is."

"Huh? My what? Abner, Collin is dead. What are you talking about?" Spencer snatched the papers from his hand. It was a DNA report on two different people that were a positive match for the same maternal and paternal DNA meaning they were siblings. "Where did you get this?"

"I took the DNA report Inspector Thompson gave me and had my friend run it against a sample of hair I took from your brush."

"What the hell for?" she shouted.

"I've had a suspicion for some time now. If you were able to find out all of this information about your family, why couldn't someone else find it too?"

"Collin's dead, Abner."

"Either he's still alive or there was another sibling we didn't know about."

"Are you kidding me with this shit?" Spencer ran her hands through her hair and growled in frustration. "My brother is out there pretending to be Jack the Ripper's ghost and killing people. I cannot believe this." She stood and paced the floor.

"I didn't believe it at first either. I had him rerun the test three times. The only way to be completely certain is to have him run the hair sample the police has directly against yours. The results would most definitely be the same unless the hair they have had been tampered with."

"Even if it had, who else knows about my family?"

"I don't know," Abner replied.

"We cannot let anyone find out about this. How much does that doctor friend of yours know?"

"Nothing. I told him it was a neighbor of mine trying to find out if she and her brother really had the same parents. Your family history has never left this room and as far as I'm concerned it never will."

"Damn you. You convinced me Inspector Thompson was our guy and I even molded him so he'd fit into my profile. You realize we're back at the very beginning, right?" Spencer said, shaking her head as she walked over to the front door.

"Where are you going?" Abner asked, watching her open it.

"For a walk. I need some air. It's broad daylight, Abner. I'll be fine." She stepped out onto the sidewalk under the gloomy sky. The sun was trying desperately to peak through the grey clouds. She was beginning to think England really was as dreadful as it looked.

She walked until the pain in her head subsided, turning her anger into sadness as tears fell down her cheeks. She spotted an empty bus stop bench and sat down. How could this have happened? How did she not know there was another brother? How could someone that shared her blood do these horrendous things to women? How in the hell did her brother find out they were related to Jack the Ripper? Her stomach turned just thinking about it.

The bus stopped in front of her with the doors opened, she shook her head and waved the driver on. When she'd first made the decision to travel to London to answer the summons, she had no idea how much her life would change. She wished she'd never opened that damn letter two months ago.

Bile rose in her throat as Spencer stood up. She bent over next to the bench, puking everything in her stomach and then some. The salty tears running down her cheeks mixed with the rancid taste in her mouth. She had forgotten her jacket and was sitting on the bench next to the puke puddle shivering in the cold wind. Her mind was hovering in a state of shock.

She jumped like a frightened cat at the feeling of someone touching her. She turned towards the warmth, realizing Abner had placed her jacket over her shoulders and was sitting close with his arm around her.

"I thought you might be cold," he said.

"I'm so lost, Abner," she replied. "I think I'm going to go back to New York on the next flight. I can't do this."

"That's not a rational decision. You can't run away now, dear girl. If anyone can stop him, it's you. I think you know that."

"We have to start all over. Everything's changed."

"Not necessarily. If anything, this may have made the game a bit easier."

"How so?"

"We have a person now, not just a ghost. We start by finding out his identity and go from there, plugging him into your profile."

"If he was able to find out our family history, he has to know about me. What if he knows I'm here working on this case?"

"There's a chance he may know who you are and possibly know you're here, but you yourself said this was a game of chess. He knows of you, but he doesn't *know* you or your moves."

"You remind me of my father, Abner. He was a smart man, but a very literal man."

"He and I may have been friends at one time had we known each other," Abner grinned.

"Do you have any children? I don't think you've ever talked about your personal life," Spencer said.

"No children. In fact, I've never been married," he replied. "But, if I'd had a child, I think I'd wish it to be someone like you."

"Thank you."

Abner cleared his throat and stood up from the bench. "Shall we get back? I do believe we have a lot of work to do."

Spencer nodded and stood. "You wouldn't happen to have any gum, would you?" she asked.

"No, but I do have breath mints," he said handing her a little tin box. "Please help yourself to as many as you see fit."

She laughed. "Is that code for my breath smells like the ass end of a horse?"

"Something like that." He grinned.

Chapter Twenty

Spencer awoke the next morning eager to get started. She dressed quickly and met Abner downstairs in the office. He was already standing by the door with his overcoat and hat on.

"We're going to the Hall of Records to see if there are any other birth records with Evelyn Porter's name on them. The last time I looked her up, I saw the records for your birth and Collin's and that was all I needed. I never thought to look for more children," he said as they walked down the street towards the parking garage. Spencer was surprised she was going along when he usually played the gentlemanly role of going to get the car himself and returning for her.

"You said we share the same paternal genes as well. Is it possible she bore multiple children with the same man? Wasn't she a common whore?"

"Yes, from everything I've found she was most definitely a prostitute. That doesn't mean she didn't have a regular customer or even a boss of some kind."

"You mean like a pimp?"

"Correct."

"Great, so my father could be a pimp." Spencer shook her head.

"It's highly possible. He would've made her abort any children or give them up as soon as they were born."

"Why doesn't my brother find and kill the pimp? He obviously channeled the wrong family tree energy and has his anger in the wrong direction."

Abner shrugged, handing the attendant his I.D. so he could enter the garage.

"So this is where you keep the cars hidden. It's very James Bond. Are you really some kind of secret special agent?" Spencer joked.

Abner rolled his eyes and lifted his chin as he walked towards his numbered parking spaces. Spencer saw the white rental car next to the yellow electric bubble on wheels as they rounded the corner.

"Maybe I should drive today," she said.

"I think not. I like my life and prefer to stay alive if you don't mind," Abner replied, getting into the driver seat of the rental car.

~

They arrived at the Hall of Records and began searching everything they could find with Evelyn Porter's name on it.

"There's no property records. She never owned anything," Abner said.

"What about her death record? Does it list any known next of kin?" Spencer asked.

"I don't know."

Abner put the property records book away and pulled out the death records book for the year of Evelyn's death. He scanned page after page until he found her death certificate.

"There's no next of kin listed. In fact, her body was identified by a woman named Barbara Phillips. Another prostitute more than likely."

"Write that name down. If she's still alive, she may know something. I've checked the hospital records before and after my birth. The only childbirth records I see are mine and Collin's."

"Do you think it's possible he wasn't born in London Proper?" Abner asked.

"Maybe."

"There is one other theory," Abner said. "What if he doesn't exist?"

"What do you mean?"

"You and Collin are fraternal twins, so your DNA would look just like the two samples we already have."

"Collin's dead, Abner."

"What if he's not?" Abner replied, taking off his reading glasses.

Spencer closed the book she was looking through and pushed her seat back from the table. "I was afraid of this. When you said the DNA was my brother my first instinct was Collin faked his death. It would give him as easy out. No one would suspect a dead guy."

"His DNA won't register on file, but his fingerprints would be in the deceased records. We'd know for sure if we had any prints from the killer."

"What if we had Collin's DNA? Even if he and I had another brother his DNA wouldn't be a complete match to Collin's so if we get Collin's DNA and compare it to the report you have, we would know for sure that he's still alive."

"How do you purpose we get a supposedly dead guys DNA?" she asked.

"Let's go back to his adopted parents. They may have something of his with hair or blood on it."

"And what do we tell them?"

"I don't know, Abner. We'll make something up on the way. Let's go," she said.

~

Abner and Spencer were greeted suspiciously when they arrived at the house of Kenneth and Barbara Rolands. Mr. Rolands led them into the parlor while Mrs. Roland made a fresh pot of tea.

"We're sorry to bother you again, but we've run across a few historical articles in connection to the research we discussed with you on our last visit and were hoping you may have a picture of Collin and possibly something that may have his DNA on it as well," Abner said.

"Are you sure this is all about some historical research? I feel like there is something you're not telling us," Kenneth replied.

"Yes, sir. There was a dress recently given to the historical society that may have Collin's grandmother's DNA on it. We would like to run it against his. We've also recovered a picture of her as well and through a computer generation program that we have in the United States we can put his picture sort of on top of hers to see if there are any identifying similarities. It's used mostly for missing children," Spencer answered.

"I see," Kenneth said.

Barbara walked into the room, setting the tea tray in the center of the table.

"They are looking for Collin's picture and something with his DNA," Kenneth informed her.

"Well, I have plenty of pictures, but I don't know how you would get his DNA. He was cremated," Barbara sighed, walking over to a cabinet on the opposite side of the room and pulling out photo album. She flipped to the back of the book and removed a picture. This is one of the last pictures that was taken of him. You can have it," she added, handing the picture to Abner.

"Do you happen to have anything of his like an old hairbrush, toothbrush, or shirt that hasn't been washed maybe? There are a number of things you can get DNA from," Spencer said.

"No, when he died we got rid of all of his stuff," Kenneth replied.

"Wait, I do have the first tooth he lost. It has dried blood on it. Will that work?" Barbara asked.

"Yes, that would be perfect," Spencer answered.

Barbara disappeared down a hallway and returned with an old pill bottle that had a small tooth inside. She handed it to Spencer.

"I had always planned to give this to him so he could share it with his own kids when they lost their first tooth."

"Thank you so much. You have both been very helpful. We will let you know if we find any results that further our research," Abner stated, shaking hands with both of them.

~

Spencer studied the picture as Abner drove them back through town to the university.

"He looks like me," she said.

"Yes. When she first handed me the photo I thought the same thing. His hair is darker, but the bone structure is very similar."

"How soon will your friend have the results?"

"Well, assuming he can extract a DNA profile from that tooth, it will take him probably a week to get the results," Abner answered.

"We have exactly nineteen days until our killer strikes again. I think we need to trace Collin's moves since his death. Maybe we can get the death certificate and work our way back from there," Spencer said.

"That's a good plan. We can go back to the Hall of Records. I think the Rolands are starting to get a little suspicious," Abner replied.

~

The next morning, Abner and Spencer arrived at the Hall of Records again.

"He obviously needed a fake identity to get out of Scotland once he faked his death there. He would've needed money to survive on all of these years too," Spencer said.

"If he had any bank accounts prior to his death, they would've transitioned to his parents. He may have set up a bank account over here and that's how he is accessing money. He may have fashioned a new passport with a new identity and easily used that to obtain a bank account and perhaps travel back and forth, but without that alias we have nothing else to go on. We need to get his death certificate and check out the circumstances surrounding his death. Unless you know his alias."

"If I were as twisted as I think he is, I'd be calling myself Jack R. Porter," Spencer said. "This is if he was able to find out our birth mother's name."

Abner grinned. "That's a very good possibility, but we can't go snooping around the banks without proper authorization and neither you nor I are of proper authority."

"No, but Inspector Thompson is." Spencer grinned.

Chapter Twenty-One

"How are we going to explain how we came up with a name?" Abner asked as they waited for the inspector to arrive.

Spencer paced the floor between their desks, spinning on her heels when it came to her.

"We'll tell him we've been putting together a list of aliases because the guy must have some way of paying his bills."

"What about the surname?"

"That's where I'm stumped," she sighed.

"We cannot arouse suspicion."

"I agree. I never want anyone to know I'm related to either of these monsters."

Abner puffed his pipe in thought. "What if we run a search on the most popular surnames in London 1888 and see where that gets us? We can add a good number of them as long as Porter happens to be one."

"Do you think Inspector Gadget will buy it? He seems to go against everything we say."

"That is indeed true, but always comes back when proven wrong," Abner replied.

Spencer shrugged. "I guess it won't hurt to run the search. We have nothing to lose…except time."

~

An hour later, Abner's printer buzzed to life in the corner. Spencer was scrolling death records in Ireland, trying to find something pertaining to Collin.

"Have a look at this," Abner said, handing her the freshly printed paper.

"I checked all over London for popular surnames in the late 19th century and Franklin and Porter weren't even in the top 150. So, I broke it down further to Greater London County and then Whitechapel itself. They're not in the top 50."

"This isn't good news," Spencer replied.

"Take a peek at this census."

Spencer scanned the paper. "You found both names?"

"Yes. It seems that neither name was very popular, but both names appear on the 1888 Census for Whitechapel. I believe it says 26 people were recorded with the surname Franklin and 19 with the surname Porter."

"Do we even know where the name Porter originated?" Spencer asked.

"No. Mildred Franklin gave Evelyn the Porter surname. Porter was probably the father's surname as well and Evelyn kept the name for you and Collin. It could have even been his given name or a nickname perhaps."

"Was Evelyn raised by Mildred?"

"I don't know the answer to that either. It could be the reason her last name is different though. She could've possibly been given to a family to raise at birth. She wouldn't really turn up on a census anywhere to be able to check it out for sure. Ladies of the night often changed hostelries, never keeping an address long enough to be added to one."

A loud knock at the door grabbed their attention.

"That'll be the inspector," Abner implied, going towards the door.

"We haven't seen you in a few days. Is there any more news on that hair they found?" Spencer asked.

"None. I'm afraid it's a dead end. The Chief has had us on street patrols. I've barely slept in the three nights past," Inspector Thompson said, pulling off his hat. "You have a message for me?"

"Actually, it's more of an inquest. We've narrowed down a list of names we'd like you to check out for possible bank accounts or other financial records," Abner replied.

"And how did you come about this list of names?"

"Whoever this person is, he's signing his name as Ripper's Ghost, therefore he believes he has a connection to JTR himself. We simply pulled a census of popular names from now, as well as Whitechapel 1888," Spencer answered as she handwrote all of the names she wanted him to check on a piece of paper. She included Porter, Franklin, and Rolands on the list of a dozen and a half names and handed it to him.

"You think he's going by Jack or Jackson as his given name?" the inspector asked, glancing at the paper. "What is the middle initial R for? Do you really believe this man is going to try and use Jack's name as his own? Legally, I mean?"

"At this point, Inspector, we don't have much to go on. So, yes, I believe he's using the Jack R. name. I many completely wrong and waste your time, but I've been right on everything else so far."

He frowned as he folded the paper, slipping it into his coat pocket. "I have a feeling I'm going on another wild goose chase."

Abner and Spencer watched him leave.

"Do you think he'll check all of the names?" Abner asked, puffing his pipe.

"No. That's why the first three are the most important."

"Smart girl," he said with a smile.

"You know what puzzles me, what was Collin doing in Dublin, Ireland and how did he supposedly die?" she sighed, going back to her computer.

"Did you find his death record?"

"No."

"His parent's said three years ago I believe, or maybe around that time. I'll check the newspapers for his name."

Spencer nodded and went back to looking at death records.

"Here it is!" he exclaimed.

"That didn't take long."

Abner read the article out loud. "Collin Rolands, a 30-year-old Englishman from Greater London, died on 1/29/2011 in a horrific, fiery car accident on R132 near Lissenhall. His remains were charred beyond recognition in the fire and he had to be identified by the rented vehicle registration and the Saint Michael pendant with CR inscribed on the back."

"Two things stick out to me right away. First, the body was charred and impossible to ID, making it easy to appear to be him based on the little bit of evidence. The family more than likely had him cremated there and his ashes flown back to London without ever questioning anything. Second, the pendant. Saint Michael is usually given to emergency workers, at least it is in the States."

"I believe some Christians follow that same practice here," Abner replied.

"Well then, I think this is proof he's had some medical training then."

"Oh, I definitely concur. He had to know the anatomy quite well to do what he's been doing." Abner relit his pipe and sat back in his squeaky desk chair.

"I know the Lissenhall area. It's north of Dublin on the way to Balbriggan." Spencer took a deep breath and sat down in her own chair. "He was looking for me, wasn't he?"

"It appears that way."

"How did he find out about me?"

"Well, he knew he was born in London's East End. There probably aren't many other baby's named Collin born in the hospitals on his birth date in that area. I'm sure he found your birth records quite easily and moved on from there."

"How the hell did he trace his roots to JTR? I mean, I wouldn't put it together unless I read the letter. You don't think there is another copy floating around somewhere do you?"

"No, I doubt it."

"Maybe he went mental when he found out his family tree was full of whores who threw their kids away," she said.

Abner shrugged. "Could be."

"I think I'm ready to call it a night." Spencer rubbed her aching temples and headed up the stairs to the flat.

Chapter Twenty-Two

A week and a half had quickly gone by with little to no word from Inspector Thompson on the name search. Spencer was started to become agitated. She wasn't a fan of the waiting game, especially when she was waiting for a killer to strike again.

"We have to do something."

"What exactly did you have in mind?" Abner asked, sipping his afternoon tea. "We can't possibly call the local banks and ask if any of the names on the list have an account there."

"I know that," she huffed, pacing the floor. Her eyes kept going back to the dry erase board with the date 11/9 circled in red. "We're running out of days."

"I know," he sighed, following her line of sight. "I have a splendid idea, let's go out for fish and chips."

Spencer turned on her heels with her head cocked to the side. "I just realized Halloween has passed. I never saw any kids trick or treating and no one came to the door."

"Oh heaven's, no. Not in this area anyway. I would imagine there weren't many out at all, with these horrendous crimes in the news lately. I did hear a man at the smoke shop making reference to JTR. It won't be long before the news hounds start piecing things together and linking these ghastly murders."

Spencer opened her mouth to reply, but a loud rapping on the door made her jump like a scared cat. Abner snickered as he moved to open the door.

"I was beginning to wonder if you'd fallen off the wagon," Spencer said.

"What exactly is meant by that? You American's baffle me," Inspector Thompson replied, removing his hat. He pulled a piece of paper from his inside coat pocket and handed it to her. "This arrived at our coroner's office three days past."

"What's taken you so long to get it to us?"

"I can't actually just take it and walk away. I had to wait for it to be analyzed for prints and so forth before acquiring a copy."

"I wondered if he was going to copy the Openshaw letter," Abner added, reading the letter for himself.

Old Boss,

That kidney fit nicely with the whore in Mitre Square, yes? I do hope you're enjoying my work. I will be sending you something grand soon. The coppers are sure to take notice this time.

Ripper's Ghost

"He doesn't reveal much. We already know the Mary Kelly murder date is coming up in a few days. That's sure to be his 'something grand', since it was JTR's masterpiece," Spencer said, handing the paper back to the inspector.

"Nothing was found on it and so far all of the postmarks have been different."

"Inspector, I've told you time and time again, he's very smart," she replied.

"How is the name search coming?" Abner asked.

Inspector Thompson sat in the chair next to Abner's desk and pursed his lips. "Dr. Montague, do you have any idea how many people with the name Jack live in England?"

Abner shrugged.

"In the last twenty years the name Jack has been at or near the top of the chart for male names. I'd guess the numbers are well into the thousands and London is no exception."

"We gave you surnames that should've narrowed the search," Spencer said.

"Yes, but again, most popular given name and popular surnames together make them just that…popular names. Either way, the search has yielded nothing."

Spencer pulled up a satellite map on her laptop. "He'll strike here next. I think we should sit and wait for him."

"How do you know for certain? That's the White's Row car park. Surely he knows there are cameras everywhere."

"Not the car park, the strip behind it, which is now a simple alleyway. It used to be Dorset street and that building right there used to be Miller's Court. That's where Mary Kelly lived. Her body was found mutilated in her own bed on November 9th,1888."

"Inspector Thompson, she is correct. This is most definitely where he will strike again," Abner added.

"He won't kill her there, but when he dumps her he will take enough time to lay everything nicely just as it had been done in Mary Kelly's room."

"This is just grand. That's only three days away," the inspector replied, moving from the chair to pace the floor. "And pray tell do you have in mind as a plan to sit and wait for him?"

Spencer printed the map and circled two spots with a red pen. "I think we sit in the car park. I know our vantage point won't be that great, but if we take the chance of sitting in the alleyway, he may notice us."

"I will put extra patrols from White's Row to Brushfield, but I can't put out an advisory for an older model dark car. We simply have too little to go on and we already have patrols searching all over greater London for this mad man."

"Where will you be?" Abner asked him.

"Patrolling the area. If you spot the car, call me. Don't do anything stupid. This man is a crazed killer."

"We'll be fine, Inspector. Just make sure you're nearby," Spencer replied.

~

The afternoon of November eighth, Abner and Spencer drove around the White's Row car park to get a feel for the area. The strong odor of coffee permeated the air inside the car.

"That dreadful stuff smells as awful as it tastes," Abner scowled, lowering his window slightly.

Spencer smiled and took another sip, before biting into her pastry.

"Yanks," Abner huffed, turning his nose up in the opposite direction.

"Where was Miller's Court actually located? It's just a large building now."

"Presumably towards that end down there, at least that's the way it looks on the old maps. I can't be certain," he answered. "The problem is the alleyway is now private and gated. I honestly doubt he will try to enter it."

"Where does that leave us then? Wait, Abner pull over." Spencer waited for the car to stop in the bus lane, before getting out and going back to the entrance to the alley from Commercial Street. "Look at this," she said as Abner caught up to her.

"The car's literally in the road. Hurry up," he chided.

"He can easily walk around this electronic gate. He may not be able to drive up and dump her, but he can still get to the spot on foot. we'll be able to catch him for sure."

"Great assessment, now come on." He started back towards the car. "We need to rest up if we're going to be back here this evening."

9 NOVEMBER 2013

Helen Dixon stepped out into the cold night air and sashayed her hips as she walked a few blocks down the street and turned the corner. It was a moonless, cloudy night and she'd just finished with her last appointment and decided to take a walk since it was still early. A black car turning around up ahead caught her attention. When the driver slowed nearby, she hiked the bottom of her skin tight dress and pulled the top down low, revealing the top half of her squished breasts and waited for it to come to a stop.

As soon as she leaned down, the locked clicked. Smiling, she checked the street and quickly opened the door. She was barely in the car when the driver grabbed her. She fought back, trying to scratch and claw her way free as he placed something wet over her face. She blacked out immediately and he shoved her limp body against the passenger door, before pulling away from the curb.

He drove through city, obeying the laws, and passing three Metro Police cars, before arriving at the abandoned building. He backed up near the side door and quickly got out to unlock it, before coming back to carry her inside to the dimly lit room. He placed her on the cold floor, stretching her limp limbs out and walked over to the steamer chest, pulling out a long bladed knife and something that resembled a paring knife.

He moved over her, placing one leg on either side of her torso, and bent down with the larger knife and in one quick slash, slit her neck in two, severing her carotid artery, slicing her larynx and cutting all way to the vertebrae. Blood sprayed the wall and dripped on the floor as she quickly bled out. Satisfied with his kill, he cut her clothes off and grabbed the paring knife as he went to work on the rest of her body.

It took him just over an hour to remove the surface of the abdomen and thighs in three separate flaps of skin and tissue and empty her abdominal cavity, careful to separate the clustered organs. He then opened her pericardium and removed her heart, cut off her breasts, and went to work gashing her face in all directions, before removing part of the nose, ears, cheeks, and eyebrows. Finally, he removed the muscles of the left thigh, striped the right thigh down to the bone, and cut a long gash down the left calf. Lastly, he made jagged cuts on both arms before cutting off the right arm.

When he was finished, he wiped the blood from his knives on a nearby towel and smiled at his handy work. He left the room and returned with a large black bag that resembled a body bag similar to the ones a coroner would use. He placed her body inside the bag and piled all of the organs into a smaller bag, seemingly used as an organ bag. He put the smaller bag into the large bag near her feet and zipped them closed. Checking the time on his pocket watch, he grinned and hurried to unlock the car and carry her out to the trunk.

He passed two Metro Police cars as he drove through the streets. Neither constable gave him a second look as he passed by. He turned onto Commercial Street and came to a stop parallel to the electronic gate to the private alleyway behind the White's Row car park. Checking the street for cars both ways, he quickly popped the trunk and grabbed the black bag, carrying it around the gate to the other side. He opened the bag and set the smaller one to the side in order to remove her body and lay it . Then, he opened the smaller bag and began hastily removing her organs, arranging them precisely.

Chapter Twenty-Three

Abner yawned as he slowed the car to turn from Brushfield to Commercial Street once again. It was nearly four a.m. and they'd been driving the same square over and over again, only seeing three other cars, two of which were Metro Police and the other being that of Inspector Thompson. They were halfway down the road when Spencer sat up straighter in her seat.

"Do you see that?"

"See what?" Abner asked, squinting to see further down the road in the darkness.

"There's a car on the side...up there. It's him!" Spencer exclaimed.

Abner grabbed his phone and rapidly dialed the inspector as he sped towards the parked car and stopped against the curb far enough away to be out of site. Spencer dove out and hurried towards the opening of the alleyway, trying to sneak up and get a good look at him.

"Inspector, we've got him. Come quick! We're at the alleyway entrance from Commercial Street. Spencer's gone to have a look...oh dear lord...NO!"

"What? Professor? What's happened?" Inspector Thompson yelled as he sped towards the alley on the opposite side, blowing through the fence and speeding in their direction.

A man lurched from the shadows, grabbing her tightly and pinning her arms to her sides as he drug her towards the black car. Pulling a wet rag from his pocket, he held it over her face as she thrashed around, easily subduing her as he shoved her inside. He squealed the tires as he sped away.

"He's taken Spencer with him," Abner shouted into the phone as the inspector floored the gas, spinning nearly out of control as he crashed through the gate on the opposite end of the alleyway.

He headed in the direction the dark car had taken towards Whitechapel Road, turning left as the taillights had also gone in that direction, but the car was out of site, leaving him clueless as to where the car went from that point. He slammed his hand hard on the dashboard and called his dispatch to have all constables look for a dark car heading in the direction of Mile End Road. Then, he turned around and went back to the scene of the crime.

Dr. Abner Montague was standing roughly fifteen feet away from the mutilated body, holding his hand over his face. He'd seen the autopsy photos from the 1888 murders, as well as the more recent ones, but nothing prepared him for seeing the actual live crime scene. Bile rose in his throat and the thought of something happening to Spencer made his chest ache as a tear slid down his cheek. The noise of a car skidding to a stop in the distance pulled his attention from the ripped up woman in front of him.

"Where has he taken her?" Inspector Thompson demanded.

"I don't know! Where were you?"

"Clearly, I was on the other side," he said sternly, pointing towards the broken gate on the other end of the alley. "Why in the bloody hell did she get out of the car?"

"I don't know. She was out before I could park. I didn't think he saw her, but he must have heard the car and was waiting in the shadows for her."

"Oh dear God!" Inspector Thompson gasped when he saw the maimed body nearby.

"You need to process this scene right away and bring me everything you find. Maybe there is something here that will lead us to Spencer."

Inspector Thompson nodded. "Did you see the tag number or make and model of the car?"

"The car emblems were missing and I was trying to write the license number down when I saw him snatch her. It was BG something," Abner was visibly shaken, thinking back to that exact moment.

"Go back to your office and look through her notes. Maybe there is something in them that will give us more to go on. I'll be in touch as soon as I know more about this…" he waved his hand towards the crime scene.

~

Driving Spencer's rental car felt odd without her in it and walking into his quiet office alone was almost too eerie for him to bear. His hands trembled as he tried to pour a cup of tea.

"You must get it together at once, Montague," he said to himself.

This was the last thing he'd ever expected and if this ghost murder really was her brother, then he'd no doubt kill her. Abner went through all of Spencer's handwritten and printed notes, but her laptop was locked with a password. He tried over a dozen combinations, but nothing worked. He was exhausted as the cloud-covered sun began to lighten the new day.

9 NOVEMBER 2013
CONTINUED

Spencer awoke in the middle of a pitch black room. The cool, damp air tingled her already heightened senses and her head pounded from the effects of the chloroform. She turned her head in the direction of heavy footsteps that seemed to be moving towards her, and stiffened with fear as she tried to move. She hadn't realized she was tied to a chair.

"You're going to be my Annie Farmer," a deep male voice stated in a low tone from somewhere nearby.

She knew not to engage a crazed killer from her training with the FBI, but she wanted to know why he was doing this.

"Who are you?" she whispered.

A match struck in the distance, making a tiny flame. She watched as the flame ignited an antique lantern, revealing a shadow of the man as he bent to set it on the ground in the corner.

"Most people refer to me as Jack, but then again, you know who I am...don't you, Spencer? I know you're helping the hounds try and stop. I've been having a jolly good time watching you all trip over your feet as I rid the streets of its dirty whores. You've seen my work. It's splendid, isn't it?" he sneered.

Spencer watched out of the corner of her eye as he stayed in the shadows of the light. She had no idea what time it was or even what day for that matter. Her stomach growled loudly as he moved around the room, coming up behind her and placing a wet rag over her face. Everything went black.

~

When Spencer awoke again, she was laying on the cold floor and the lantern was still burning. A plate of some sort of bread, a plastic cup of water, and a metal bucket were against the wall. The room seemed to be made of concrete and the door and doorframe were some sort of metal. She tried the handle, but it was locked and a deadbolt above it was more than likely locked as well. She moved back to the plate and ate the stale bread, barely chewing, and drank the lukewarm water in one long swallow. Assuming the bucket was to be used as a toilet, she quickly relieved herself.

A few minutes later, she suddenly became extremely tired and could barely stand up, so she sat down on the floor near the warm lantern and closed her eyes. When she opened them again, she was tied to the chair once more in the darkness.

Chapter Twenty-Four

Abner sat at his desk with a sorrowful look on his face. He'd spent the last four and a half days going over all of Spencer's notes and had found nothing indicating where the killer had taken her. He'd barely eaten and only slept here and there when exhaustion set in.

It took him twice as long as normal to answer the pounding on the door.

"I'm sorry it has taken me so long to get this to you. With the latest development, I had to inform the chief of yours and Ms. Donovan's assistance on this case," Inspector Thompson said, removing his hat. "Needless to say, he was angered and threatened my badge, but after a heated conversation, he realized without the assistance of the criminologist, we probably wouldn't know as much as we do now."

"Where does this leave us with the investigation?"

"He's pulled every constable off holiday and put them in the streets. He wants this man stopped at all costs. We will find her, Abner."

"I know. I only hope we find her alive and in one piece."

"Here's the file on the grotesquely mutilated woman. How someone could do such a thing to another human being is beyond me."

"Jack the Ripper was fueled by hatred, a very deep hatred. This man who calls himself Ripper's Ghost...," he sighed. "Is another story altogether. I'm afraid I have no idea why he is doing what he's doing."

Abner opened the folder on his desk and began going over the autopsy of the deceased woman. She was no doubt the killer's Mary Kelly. His stomach churned as he skimmed over the pictures and read through the notes. Helen Dixon was her name and she was just under thirty years old, with fair skin and hair. The last person to see her was a neighbor at the brothel around one in the morning.

"He was careful not to cut himself. We've only found her DNA," the inspector added.

"He's most definitely skilled in medical studies of some sort, either through university or possibly acquired on his own. One thing is for certain, he's staying directly in line with our timeline." Abner closed the file and walked over to a folder on Spencer's desk, pulling out the timeline notes she'd printed from her computer. "Annie Farmer was the next victim in 1888. Mary Kelly was the last of the canonical five, which were assumed to be Jack the Ripper, but this new killer is following the Whitechapel murders, not just JTR. Maybe he assumed JTR was responsible for all of the murders and attacks, either way, Annie Farmer was found on the 21st of November with a shallow cut on her throat...alive."

"Unless you know where he has taken her, there's no other option, but to wait and see what happens," Inspector Thompson said.

"We can't just sit and wait! Have you gone mad?" Abner smacked the top of the desk, causing Inspector Thompson to jump with surprise.

"Calm down, Professor."

"Ms. Donovan is in the hands of this lunatic killer, and you want to sit and wait. Wait for what? Him to slice her to pieces?"

"You said it yourself, the next victim was found alive."

Abner couldn't very well tell him that the killer was Spencer's brother, and if he did indeed know who she was, he'd most definitely deviate from the plan and kill her.

"Inspector Thompson, it is well documented that Annie Farmer more than likely faked her attack in 1888. She had apparently stolen from a potential customer and when he became angry, she cut herself with a blunt object and began screaming that he was Jack the Ripper. The police were skeptical and the investigation was called off."

"What exactly does this mean?"

"Our killer may skip right over portion of the Whitechapel Timeline."

"Alright. Who's next on the list?" Inspector Thompson asked.

"Here lies the next problem. Rose Mylett was strangled and found in Clark's Yard on the 20th of December 1888. There were mixed feelings about her death. Some say she fell in a drunken stupor and accidentally hung herself on her dress."

Inspector Thompson made a note on his pocket-sized notebook. "Next?"

"That's it, I'm afraid. The next murder wasn't reported for nearly six months, when Elizabeth Jackson's body parts were found in the Thames in May and June of 1889."

"Bloody Hell," the inspector cursed, shaking his head. "Where does this leave us?"

"I'm not a criminologist, Inspector. I'm a history professor and a true crime author. I simply do not know."

"Were there any other murders or attacks in the original timeline that this ghost skipped over?"

"Yes," Abner said, flipping through the pages. "Ah, here it is. Emma Smith. She was assaulted and possibly robbed by two or three men on the 3rd of April 1888 and reported one of them being very young. She died the next day as a result of being stabbed in the vagina, which ruptured her peritoneum, causing peritonitis. It's uncertain whether or not she knew her attackers, but no description was given."

"Should I go back and check the hospital records to see if our ghost copied this one?"

Abner lifted his chin in thought. "That's a grand idea. If in fact he did, then that will give us an idea of what to expect next."

"What area should we be looking in?"

Abner pulled up the map and began piecing together the 1888 location with the current map. "Emma Smith was attacked at the junction of Brick Lane and Osborn Street, near Wentworth Street. Check police reports for that area around the 3rd or 4th of April. Also, check with the Royal London Hospital. That's the closest one and she may have been taken there. We're looking for a women with vaginal blunt trauma, not necessarily a stabbing."

"Splendid," Inspector Thompson said, hurrying out the door.

16 NOVEMBER 2013

Spencer wasn't sure how long she'd been held captive. She was tired and very weak, too weak to move, which was why she was no longer tied to the chair. A couple slices of bread and a glass of water per day had made her body starved and dehydrated. She could barely open her eyes when the dark shadow crossed the room without looking directly at her. She couldn't believe her own flesh and blood could this to her and wondered if he actually knew the truth.

"How much longer are you going to keep me here?" she whispered.

He went about his task of changing her toilet bucket and tossing some bread on the plate nearby, without ever acknowledging her words, almost as if he was on autopilot.

Spencer huddled further into the corner, shivering from the cool air in the room mixing with the cold cement floor under her. She wondered why he hadn't killed her yet. Had he done this to all of his victims? Held them captive? She tried to remember what he'd said to her when he first grabbed her, as she watched his shadow leave the dimly lit room. The door slammed shut with an eerie thud. She wasn't sure how much time she had before the antique oil lamp would run out of fuel. She knew he was drugging her, keeping her sedated most of the time, but she quickly ate the stale bread and drank the water anyway.

Chapter Twenty-Five

Abner was looking at the calendar and pacing the floor with his pipe in his hand when Inspector Thompson arrived a few days later.

"What on earth has taken so long?" Abner asked, opening the door.

The inspector walked inside, removing his hat. "I checked our reports and there were no similar attacks listed for either of those days in April. The hospital didn't have any reports, but one of the nurses said a woman from the street had come in complaining that she'd been raped by a man and was in severe pain. She was gone when the nurse came back into check on her. The name she gave was Sandra Brown and the address she gave turned out to be a restaurant. I've been all over the streets trying to find her, but no one knows who she is."

"This could be his work, but it may not be. These women of the night go through a lot of trouble to stay off the radar."

"I even went through the unidentified body listing and no females had been reported that week."

"If he did attack a woman around that time, you may never find her anyway. Especially, if she lived," Abner replied, puffing his pipe.

"This next victim on the timeline…where was she found?"

"Thrawl Street, near the Brick Lane Police Station, actually. Back in 1888 George Street was in that area. Many of the Whitechapel murder victims lived in that area and on that street, including some of JTR's victims."

"Surely you don't think he will leave her right there, do you?"

Abner shrugged. "He's been pretty spot on so far."

"I'll contact the station and have them put out an extra patrol tonight in the area."

Abner grabbed his coat and hat from the rack.

"Where are you off to?" The inspector asked.

"Church. I believe a lot of praying is in order."

"God, help us all," Inspector Thompson said, walking out the door behind him.

21 NOVEMBER 2013

Spencer was asleep on the cold damp floor when he walked in. He grabbed her, holding a wet rag over her face until she went limp against him. He grabbed the thin blade from his pocket and a made a shallow cut across the front of her throat, watching as a thin line of blood trickled down her neck. Then, he carried her out to the trunk of his car.

The Metro Police were thicker in the streets than they had been the last time he was out and he wondered if the hounds were finally on his trail. He turned down Thrawls Street, passing the police station, then turned again on onto Commercial Street. It was just after two a.m. when he circled back around and deposited Spencer's body onto the sidewalk in the shadows, before disappearing into the night.

Chapter Twenty-Six

Inspector Thompson pounded frantically on the door at 27 White Church lane. "Dr. Montague? Professor!" he shouted.

Abner fumbled his way down the stairs in the darkness to answer the door and was nearly run over as the inspector raced inside.

"She's been found!" he screeched.

"Spencer? "

"Yes! She's unconscious at the moment, but alive. I just left the Royal London Hospital."

"When? Where was she found? What time is it?" Abner asked, trying to get his bearings. He's been unable to sleep most of the night and had finally passed out from pure exhaustion. His adrenaline was slowing starting to kick in. "I need to go to her," he said, hurrying up the stairs to change clothes and forgetting the inspector was downstairs.

Inspector Thompson dialed the number to the hospital as he waited for the professors return. A few minutes later, Abner appeared freshly dressed in a suit.

He grabbed his hat and coat from the rack before noticing the inspector sitting in his chair.

"Good heavens!" he gasped. "I thought you'd gone."

"I just rang the hospital. She hasn't woken up yet. She was severely drugged and very malnourished. Her throat has also been cut."

"My God! How is she alive?" Abner exclaimed, rushing out the door to get into the inspectors waiting car.

"The wound is only superficial. She has ligature marks around her arms, legs, and chest. More than likely he kept her bound to something. A chair perhaps," Inspector Thompson said as he drove through the dark streets.

Abner checked the time on his pocket watch. It was just after four a.m. "When was she found?"

"Roughly an hour ago. I got the call that an unconscious woman had been found on Thrawl Street and was taken directly to the hospital. I headed there straight away."

"Why didn't you ring me?"

"I wasn't sure what I'd find, honestly. I almost didn't recognize her when they asked me to ID her. She's in dreadful shape, but she is most definitely alive."

They arrived at the hospital and hurried into the emergency department. The nurse told them she'd been moved up to the critical care unit, so they rode the lift to the third floor. it was eerily quiet with dim lighting when they stepped off. A small waiting room was on the corner near the lift and the nurse's station was further down, near the middle of the hallway.

"I'm Detective Inspector Shane Thompson and this is Dr. Abner Montague. We're here to see about Spencer

Donovan, the young woman who was brought in earlier this morning."

"Yes, Inspector, she's right this way. I'll have her doctor come talk to you," she said, showing them to room number three.

Abner gasped as he took in the sight of the young woman. Spencer looked gangly. Her face was sunken in and her skin was very pale. A thin white bandage ran along her neck under her jaw and an oxygen tube was shoved into her nostrils. She had an IV line in each arm and other leads coming from the top of her hospital gown and connecting to machines next to the bed. A thick blanket covered most of her body from the shoulders down.

He moved closer, running the back of his knuckles over her soft cheek.

"You poor child. You've been through hell," he whispered.

Both men turned around when the door to the room opened behind them.

"Inspector, I'm Dr. Thaddeus Patel," the balding man in the white lab coat stuck his hand out.

"Dr. Patel, this is Ms. Donovan's colleague, Dr. Abner Montague."

Abner shook the doctor's hand, before turning back to look at Spencer once more.

"We found traces of Trichloromethane and a large concentration of Phenobarbital and Diazepam in her system, which can be a very deadly cocktail. She's stable, which means she will wake up when the levels in her bloodstream begin to drop."

"What are the common names?" Inspector Thompson asked. "I know Trichloromethane is chloroform, but

197

what's in the cocktail? What are those drugs commonly used for?"

"Luminal, the common name for Phenobarbital, is a seizure drug and Valium or Diastat, common names for Diazepam, is used to treat a number of things from panic attacks to restless leg syndrome. They're both sedatives and should never be taken together."

Inspector Thompson made a few notes in his notepad before tucking it back into his jacket pocket.

"Any idea when she might wake up?" Abner asked.

Dr. Patel pursed his lips and shook his head. "It could be hours or days. The drugs in her system are at a dangerous level, but it's gone down nearly 5% since she arrived. We're giving her nutrients through one IV and the other is giving her a saline solution to help flush it out of her system."

~

Abner stayed at her bedside for the next twenty four hours and Inspector Thompson dropped in or rang periodically to check on her status. Spencer finally awoke, very groggy and extremely weak.

The first feeling she felt when she opened her eyes in the dimly lit room was warmth. She relaxed into the warmth surrounding her, sure she'd finally died. It wasn't until Abner appeared in her face that she realized she was alive and in the hospital.

"Oh, thank God," she whispered.

"You're going to be okay. Let me go get the doctor," Abner said, rushing out of the room, returning a few minutes later with a balding man in a white lab coat.

Dr. Patel turned on the overhead lights, illuminating the room. Spencer quickly closed her eyes and shook her head as the searing brightness penetrated through her eyelids.

"Turn it off," she whispered hoarsely.

"I'm sorry," Dr. Patel said, turning the light back down. He moved to her beside, checking her pupils with his penlight and looking at the readout on the monitors. "You're very lucky to be alive."

"I feel like I'm on my death bed," she said.

Abner stood at her other side, offering her ice chips to suck on.

"You were drugged very heavily. It's going to take some time for the remainder of the sedative to wear off."

"Is there someone you want me to call back home?" Abner asked softly.

"No," she answered.

"I know your parents are gone, but a friend perhaps?"

"No, Abner. There's no one."

He nodded and squeezed her hand for his own comfort.

A nurse walked into the room and took a vile of blood. Inspector Thompson burst through the door behind her, rushing up next to Dr. Patel.

"How are you feeling?" he asked.

"Like I've been to hell and back," she replied.

"I'll leave you alone for a bit. It's best that you get some rest. the only way to get the drugs out of your system is to sleep them off. We'll try solid foods tomorrow, but for now you're on a liquid diet," Dr. Patel said.

Spencer waited for the door to close behind him.

"How long was I gone?" she asked.

"Twelve days," Abner replied.

"Where did he take you? Did you see what he looked like?" Inspector Thompson questioned.

"Slow down, Inspector. She's just endured the worst two weeks of her life."

"Abner it's okay. We need to catch this son of a bitch," she sighed. "It was hell. Absolute hell. I was in a cold dark room with cement or concrete floors and walls, with no light except for an old oil lantern that he lit when he fed me, which was a couple slices of bread and a cup of water. I only remember eating maybe four or five times, so he must have kept me drugged for most of it. The room was in a building of some sort. It smelled musty."

"What did he look like?"

"I barely saw him." She shook her head. "He stayed in the shadows when he was in the room. Based on his shadow and what I did see of him, he's around average height and build, but very strong. He has dark hair and his face is kind of scruffy like he needed a shave. He always had a fedora on his head."

"What about his voice?" Inspector Thompson asked.

"Raspy," she replied, then it dawned on her. He'd spoken. "He said something to me, but I can't remember. He only spoke once."

Abner sighed.

"What? Did he kill someone else?"

"No. You were the next girl on the list or put in place of her anyway. Do you remember our timeline of the Whitechapel murders?"

Spencer shook her head. The drugs had done a number on her and everything was fuzzy.

"Annie…"

"That's it. He said I was his Annie…something."

"Farmer," Abner finished. "Annie Farmer. She was the one who was found alive with her throat cut…"

Spencer reached up to her throat, skimming her fingers over the bandage.

"It's okay. The doctor said it's only superficial and probably won't leave much of a scar," he said, patting her hand.

"What about his car? Did you notice anything about it?" Inspector Thompson asked.

"No. I don't remember being in his car at all. He must've drugged me or something."

"There was chloroform in your system. That's what he's using to keep the girls quiet," the inspector sighed.

"He's using an old warehouse or building of some sort. There's probably no electricity there either," she stated as she closed her eyes. The effect of the drugs was back, causing her to brain to go fuzzy again.

"Get some rest. I'm not going anywhere." Abner patted her hand again. "Dr. Patel said you'd be in and out until it was completely out of your system."

"It was dark…so dark and very…very cold," she murmured as she dozed off.

Inspector Thompson shook his head. "His bloody arse is going to pay for what he did to her when I find him."

Abner smiled softly.

"You know, you were at the top of our suspect list for a little while. It's good to know I can cross you off now."

Inspector Thompson stepped back, puffing up his chest. "Me? What in God's name for?"

"She's damn good at what she does and she can make anyone fit into the box if she wants them to. She even made it look easy," Abner replied.

Inspector Thompson shook his head. "I don't understand how."

"It's very easy to disguise a look, a voice, even one's own height. She knows the tricks of the trade inside and out. Finding your hair in the box with that kidney threw up a huge flare."

"Well, for my sake, I'm glad she came to her senses. Do you happen to know why she's no longer working for the FBI?"

"No. It's not in her record and she's never talked about it."

"It's a shame they lost someone as good as she is," he sighed. "I need to get back on the street. I'll check in with you in a bit."

Chapter Twenty-Seven

Two days later, Spencer checked herself out of the hospital against the doctor's orders. Abner wasn't sure what to do or say. He'd never met anyone as headstrong as the stubborn yank sitting at the desk across from him.

"What?" Spencer asked.

"Nothing," Abner replied.

"I don't need to be cooped up in a hospital. I spent twelve damn days in a ten by ten room in the pitch black. I think I'll be fine eating and sleeping here."

Abner shrugged. She did have a good point. The doctor had informed him to bring her back to the emergency room if she began puking or convulsing with a fever. The drug levels had gone down tremendously and the withdrawals were what he was worried about and why he wanted to keep her in the hospital. So far, she'd been fine.

"I still think you should go back to the states and let Scotland Yard catch him," Abner finally said.

"What?" Spencer spun around in her chair to face him. "You've got to be kidding me. Scotland Yard can't find their way out of a wet paper bag. Without our help, they'd still be sipping their damn afternoon tea while he goes on killing more women. You've read the files. The Whitechapel murders went on until 1891," she exclaimed.

"I think it's unsafe for you to be here. What if he comes for you again?"

"I'm almost certain he knew who I was and he could have easily killed me then. He's my own flesh and blood and damn it, I'm going to stop him. Can we please move on?"

Abner nodded without saying anything else about quitting the case to the stubborn yank.

Spencer went on. "From the picture we have of Collin, it's definitely him, although he's aged a lot since that picture was taken."

"I hate to go back to the Rolands, but I wonder if Collin was ever on seizure medication," Abner stated. "That's what he was sedating you with. A cocktail of seizure and anxiety meds."

"If we go back they are going to know something's up and if we ask Inspector Gadget to pull his medical record, he'll know something's up," she huffed. "I say we move on. We know it's him and without his alias, we won't be able to track his medical prescriptions anyway."

"You have a good point," Abner puffed his pipe.

Spencer was surprised at how much she'd grown accustomed to the smell of cherry tobacco. She definitely preferred it over the stale, musty scent of the room she'd been held in.

~

Spencer and Abner spent the next few days going over everything once again, focusing on an area that would be a good location for Collin to work from. Thanksgiving had come and gone with her in the hospital and the first week of December had already passed as well.

"We have a little over two weeks before he strikes again," Abner stated, between sips of his afternoon tea.

"I know. Rose Mylett, 20th of December, strangled with a string in Clarke's Yard," she replied, sounding more like the game Clue.

Abner tried to hide his snicker.

"Maybe we should go over there and check it out."

"I don't know if that's a grand idea," he replied. "It could be a long shot anyway." The last thing he wanted to do was take her near the killer again.

"There is one other thing I've been thinking about. I know I'm grasping at straws here, but if he really does know about our bloodline, I might have an idea about where he is."

"What do you mean?" Abner asked, setting his tea cup down.

"He's stuck in the past. I honestly wouldn't be surprised if he was driving a horse and carriage to be honest with you. The building he had me in was very old. There were no windows, it was made of some sort of cement or brick, and there was no running water. It's inhabitable, but I believe he may be living there himself."

"You think maybe it's a building one of your family members lived in?"

Spencer nodded. "Honestly, yes."

"I think you may be on to something. Let's pull the last known address for all of the women in your family tree and work our way back," Abner said.

"Are you finished with your tea?" Spencer asked, knowing he hated for his tea time to be interrupted.

"My tea can wait. We're running out of time and must get start on these addresses straight away."

Spencer smiled and booted her laptop back up.

~

It was well after midnight when Spencer and Abner finally had the list completed. They weren't completely sure of any of the addresses since none of the women stayed anywhere long enough to be claimed on a census. The areas that Abigail Bigsby and Abigail Franklin may have lived no longer had streets.

"All of the areas around these old addresses are now markets or other businesses that have been erected literally on top of the old streets. I'm afraid it may be a dead end," Abner said, trying not to yawn.

"I agree, but what about Mildred and Evelyn? We know Evelyn's address, at least around the time of my birth. It's written on the hospital records, but again, it may be false."

"That building is still standing. It was a women's shelter back in the eighties and has since been turned into rental flats. The only person we are missing is Mildred." Abner sat back in his chair with an odd expression on his face.

Spencer moved to turn her computer off and Abner abruptly smacked the top of his desk, causing her to jump from her seat.

"Her death record!" he exclaimed.

"What about it? It's right here," she replied, shuffling the papers on her desk.

"Let me have a look," he said, moving around his desk to get the paper. "Ah, as I suspected. She died in 1966 and record keeping was more precise. Her address is listed on here. I'm not sure how true it is, knowing she was a lady of the night and probably changed addresses many times over."

"Let me see it, I'll pull it up on the map on the computer and see if it still exists."

After a few quick key strokes the address popped up on the screen. Abner and Spencer pulled up the satellite image and noticed the abandoned building right away.

"It looks like a dilapidated old warehouse of some sort," Abner said.

"This has to be it. Look, it's in Spitalfields just as I said it would be," she exclaimed.

"Here it is on the map in 1950. It looks as though it's always been a dreadful area of town."

"I bet it was a whorehouse back then, or at least a place that rented rooms to the women of the streets."

"Oh, I'm sure of it," he replied. "I say we take a drive over there at first light."

"I thought you didn't want me going anywhere near him," she teased.

"I never said we were getting out of the car."

~

The next morning, Spencer sipped her coffee as Abner drove her rental car through the streets of London where the women in her family had lived, worked, and eventually died. She had a very surreal, yet somber feeling as she watched the buildings pass by. The car finally came to a stop on the side of the road in a very dingy area that was once a bustling warehouse district.

"The address is up ahead on the left. I'm going to make a pass by. See if you notice his dark car," Abner said, pulling away from the curb.

Spencer looked at the rundown building. There were no windows and it appeared to be made of brick. She had an eerie feeling creep through her as they drove by.

"This is it," she said. 'I don't see the car, but there could be a back entrance."

Abner continued down the road and turned on a side street, before coming to a stop behind an old building one block over. He left the engine running in case they needed to make a hasty exit and clicked the power locks one more time for safety.

"You had better ring the inspector and tell him to meet us here straight away," he exclaimed. He wasn't too keen on being in this area of town for long, Especially not with a madman on the loose.

~

Inspector Thompson arrived a short time later with another detective and two constables. Abner drove around to the warehouse and parked next another old building out of site.

"Are you certain this is where he held you captive?" he questioned.

"Yes. I'd bet my life on it."

"You two wait here and lock the doors. Ring my cell number if you see him or the car."

Inspector Thompson and his men moved on foot towards the building as Spencer and Abner watched from a few hundred yards away.

"Do you think he's in there?" Abner asked.

Spencer shrugged. "Who knows. If he is…I hope they kill him."

Abner nodded.

"When this whole thing first began, I was eager to see what was driving him to do this. Then, after I found out he was my brother, I wanted to know him. Now, after spending twelve days in hell with him, I honestly just want him dead."

"Is that smoke?" Abner exclaimed, squinting his eyes to get a better look.

Chapter Twenty-Eight

The building was pitch black and smelled strongly of lamp oil when the inspector and his men entered. They drew their guns and shined their flashlights as they made their way further inside and down a short hallway with a few doors on the left side. Inspector Thompson tried the handle on the first door and it opened into a small room. He shined his light all around as he walked inside. There was nothing in the room except an old steamer trunk.

He opened the lid and gasped when he saw the array of knives laying neatly across the bottom. He wasn't sure if the killer was still in the building, so he whispered for his men to come into the room as he flashed his light on the contents of the trunk for them to see. He used his phone to take multiple pictures of the room and the trunk before moving on.

They left the door open and went into the next room. It was similar in size to the first and completely bare, except for a chair and a bucket. Inspector Thompson had a good feeling this was where Spencer had been held. He quickly snapped a few pictures and ushered the men towards the last door at the end of the hallway.

All of the men gasped and jumped back when they shined their lights into the room. A rectangle metal table was in the center of the room with various surgical knives and hand saws lined up on a towel that was laying on a smaller metal table nearby. The room was nearly twice the size of the others. Inspector Thompson noticed the larger table was similar to an autopsy table, but it was beveled and had two drains in the center. He took over a dozen photos of the room, tables, and other equipment.

The men began making their way out of the building when one of them noticed the hallway wall was covered with photos and newspaper clippings. Inspector Thompson saw the name Jack the Ripper on many of them as he took photos of the wall.

The sound of smashing glass came from the end of the hallway. Inspector Thompson raced towards the sound with his gun drawn and his flashlight illuminating the narrow corridor. His men were on his heels as they entered the far room.

"You've found me. Well done, Inspector," A deep voice resonated from the shadows. "Although, I do believe you have Ms. Donovan to thank."

Inspector Thompson shined his light, looking all around the room for the person speaking, when another glass smashed and a bright flame lit up the room. He saw the man laying in a pool of blood on the opposite side of the table as flames spread around the room. One of his men snapped a photo of the dead man before they ran out of the room. The searing flames raced up the hallway behind them, lighting up the floor and walls. By the time they reached the exit, the entire building was engulfed in flames and beginning to crumble to the ground.

~

Abner and Spencer raced towards the men who were hunched over, coughing and gasping for breath. One of them came out with part of his clothing on fire and Abner patted him down to put it out.

"Good heavens!" Abner exclaimed. The sound of the fire department sirens was getting louder in the distance.

"You were right," Inspector Thompson gasped to Spencer. "He was in there. He started the fire and slit his own throat."

"Oh my God," she whispered.

The fire engines arrived and went to work trying to douse the blaze, but the building was too far gone and had begun to crumble. Three police cars turned down the street with their lights flashing and sirens wailing.

"There's more...I'll fill you in on the details later," Inspector Thompson wheezed as one of the medics check him over.

"We should probably get going," Abner said, nodding towards the police cars heading in their direction.

"I agree," she replied, heading hastily towards the car which was still parked out of sight.

~

Three days later, Spencer and Abner were sitting in the flat playing cards when Inspector Thompson knocked on the door. Spencer raced down the stairs towards the

212

door and Abner followed, albeit in a slightly more refined manner.

"I'm sorry it has taken me so long. The inquisition finally ended this morning." He removed his hat. "The Chief Inspector had more questions than I had answers, but in the end the case was closed."

He stuck his hand out to Spencer. "I owe you a hefty bit of gratitude, Ms. Donovan and the Chief has asked me to thank you for him as well. He would have met with you personally, but he is now headed to a meeting I was not privy to."

"No thanks is necessary, Inspector. In a sense, I was only doing my job," she replied, shaking his hand. "I only wish we could have found him sooner."

"Speaking of find something," he said, handing her a thick accordion style folder. "Here is the fire investigation report and a copy of all of the pictures that were taken. I thought you might want to close your own case, so to speak."

"Thank you," she said, sitting in her desk chair and opening the file.

"Was it him for sure?" Abner asked. "Did you get an ID?"

"The body was badly burned, but they were able to extract a partial DNA sample to compare with the hair from the kidney box. It was enough of a match to say it was the same person, but I didn't hear the exact numbers. So, to answer your question, yes it was him, but I don't think we will ever know who he was. The DNA profile is not in any system that we've checked."

Spencer looked through the dozens of pictures, stopping when she came across the chair in the room.

"This is where he had me." She handed the photo to Abner.

"Yes, I presumed it was," Inspector Thompson replied. "There is a picture of him in there that one of the constables took, but the room was already engulfed and all you really see is the body of a man dressed in dark clothes with a pool of blood under him. The bright flames distorted the face."

Spencer perused the pictures until she came to the one he was talking about. She felt relief seeing his body and knowing he was dead. She'd asked to see the body after the autopsy, but the it had been so badly burned there wasn't much left and what was left had been charred too badly to autopsy. The coroner did however say that the carotid artery had been severed, which was the most probable cause of death.

"What about the car?" she asked.

"The car had traces of all of the victims blood in the trunk, as well as traces of your blood and hair. A few pieces of hair were found on the driver seat which also match the ones from the kidney box," he paused. "What I cannot seem to understand is why didn't he kill you? It also puzzles me how he not only knew your name, but he also knew you were assisting on this case. He mentioned that I should thank you for helping me, just before he cut his own throat."

Spencer felt an eerie chill run up her spine. "He was a very intelligent man, Inspector. He may have been onto you and following you the entire time, but since he's dead, we'll probably never know."

"You bring a good point. I hate to bid you both farewell, but I have other meetings of my own to attend this afternoon." Inspector Thompson placed his hat back on his head. "Ms. Donovan, perhaps we could have a cup of tea before you venture back across the pond."

"Perhaps," she replied with a smile.

As soon as the inspector was gone, Spencer dumped out the file onto her desk. "Checkmate," she exclaimed with a grin.

"It's probably a good thing he cooked himself," Abner said.

"That's true, but he left a lot of unanswered questions," she sighed. "No one can ever know about my family or this case." She took all of her and Abner's notes and shoved them neatly into the large file with the inspector reports and pictures.

"I agree. As far as I'm concerned, case closed," Abner stated.

"Case closed," she replied, nodding her head.

SIX MONTHS LATER

Spencer was sitting on the couch in her apartment, petting Alfred, her gray and white cat. The evening news was about to begin on the TV and the fresh cup of coffee on the table had steam rising from the top. She'd finally gotten used to being home and was looking forward to figuring out her next career path. Being a prosecutor had its good and bad points, but working the case in London had also reminded her of the good and bad points of being a criminologist.

A loud knock at the door caused the cat to shoot off of her lap and scurry through the apartment to hide under her bed.

"Who could that be?" she said aloud as she walked over to the door.

"I'm looking for Ms. Spencer C. Donovan."

"You got her."

"I need to see your ID, please."

"What the hell for?"

"I have a confidential package for you."

"Hold on." Spencer closed and locked the door, returning a minute later with her NY driver's license.

He checked the picture and the name, then had her sign on two different lines before handing her the thick envelope. He wasn't even in the elevator when she sat on the couch and tore the package open. She pulled out a letter, a printed article and a newly dated newspaper clipping.

Ms. Donovan,

I hope this letter finds you well. I know you implied that you did not wish to return to London anytime soon, but I thought you might be interested in our latest news. Read the article before you read the news clipping.

Ring me with your flight information.

Regards,
Abner Montague, PH.D

"Flight information? You've lost your mind old man," she laughed and began reading the historical article from 1889. The paper slipped from her hands as she reached for the news clipping. After reading it, she checked the date. It had been written three weeks prior.

~

Abner Montague was sipping his afternoon when the phone rang loudly. He reached for it and answered without missing a beat.

"Only a stubborn yank would interrupt my afternoon tea," he huffed.

"My flight arrives at eight p.m. tomorrow," Spencer said. "And leave that damn banana bubble on wheels at home," she growled before hanging up.

"It was nice chatting with you as well," he replied to the dial tone.

About the Author

Kennedy Welles has lived in the south all of her life, but often travels north for the snow and scenic mountains. She enjoys reading multiple genres and writing mystery and suspense stories of her own. She's also a history buff, so many of stories involve actual historic events.